Sumner Carnahan has collaborated with composers, performers, and artists for decades to present her writing "off the page." She was born in Corpus Christi, Texas, and lives in Santa Fe. She has six books in print and numerous recordings of her work. This is her first novel.

BURNING BOOKS · SANTA FE NEW MEX · MMXI

Only a Messenger

Sumner Carnahan

A QUADRANTS SERIES NOVEL

ONLY A MESSENGER © 2011 Melody Sumner Carnahan
THE QUADRANTS SERIES © 2011 Burning Books

All rights reserved. This book may not be reproduced, in whole or in part, for any reason, or by any means now existing or yet to be developed, without consent in writing from the author.

EDITING, DESIGN, AND PRODUCTION: Burning Books

THE AUTHOR WISHES TO THANK THE FOLLOWING FOR EDITORIAL ADVICE AND ASSISTANCE:
Diane Armitage, Aline Brandauer, Thomas Frick, Marianne Kuntz, Lynn Larsen, Ed Oppenheimer, Slim Randles, Mitch Rayes, Michael Schippling, Sheila Davies Sumner, Sarah Skenazy, and Tracy Wein.

BOOK AND COVER DESIGN: Michael Sumner

ISBN: 978-0-936050-34-8 limited edition paperback

INQUIRIES MAY BE ADDRESSED TO THE PUBLISHER:
Burning Books, P. O. Box 2638, Santa Fe, NM 87504, www.burningbooks.org; or to the author at: www.sumnercarnahan.org

DISTRIBUTION: Small Press Distribution, www.spdbooks.org

Published and printed in the United States of America.

contents

Summary Abstract 11

Notebooks 1995: David Ambrose Gentry ... 17

Notebooks 1996: D.A.G. 33

Colibri's Diary: Mexico 1992–1996 57

Notebooks 1997–1998: D.A.G. 101

Colibri's Diary: California 1996–1998 119

Notebooks 1998–1999: D.A.G. 137

Notebooks 2000: D.A.G. 151

Notebooks 2001: D.A.G. 189

Only a Messenger

Summary Abstract

At first he decided to devote his life to finding her killer.

He sits in the back of the café under dark wood beams drinking coffee from a paper cup. The owner at a nearby table scowls as if to say, You've had your moment, now you must go.

His bereavement is an affront to the complacency of others.

Colibri. She wasn't like a wife. She was like no one else in the world.

What is sin, David?

A game we play.

Do you remember the name of this little yellow flower?

At the moment of her death he was watching a special report on television. The great fire at Mortem Fendano Botanical Library in Bogotá. Suspected arson. The use of unusual plasma explosives. The library housed the most comprehensive collection of generative plant material from endangered or extinct species in the Western Hemisphere.

He had their plane tickets in his pocket. Had

just picked them up that day. He and Colibri were to arrive in Bogotá later that week for a one-year stipend from UCSD. Working, as a team, in recovery of plant DNA. He hadn't heard her scream. She was dead when he got to her. Slumped in the doorway to the building. He had gotten up to investigate when a neighbor rang the bell.

The police were useless. There were no witnesses. No clear motive. She wasn't robbed or raped.

She had no enemies.

He had studied to become a scientist but that was behind him now. Convinced of the great ugliness of human beings, with their obscenely arrogant posturing, his heart is frozen. He attempts another dimension by going inside himself. He sleeps on a futon by the door. The curtains are stained and the panes of his windows smudged with soot. He wears earplugs all the time except while listening to music in his room.

What you perceive in the rift between the mental and the sensual is alive, is potential. Advice from his mentor, Monroe, who speaks to him from books and audio recordings.

There was the letter she never received. About a meeting with Raúl, her long lost brother, running guns and god knows what in Mexico. And there were the seeds. Packets of seeds confiscated during an FBI investigation.

He knows we are composed of immortal elements. Hydrogen oxygen nitrogen carbon. Carbon, though, is a problem. It is why we are so frequently dissatisfied. Carbon too readily combines and steadily declines. Perhaps, he reasons, it is the subatomic realm that gives rise to a feeling of the sublime. The infinite hides there. Eternity. No way to reach a conclusion. Concussion. The stated cause of her death. End of the line. End of time for her. The largest array of interstellar spacetime cannot contain the pain he feels right now.

He sees how the tabletop is gouged in spots, as if it had once been used as a chopping block. His father had been a brutal man who drank excessively while managing control of a successful investment company. His mother often protected her son, but eventually her weakness overcame her strength. She knew the man she'd married was flawed, but she had hoped her love could master him. Finally, she had to leave. The man tried everything to get her back. She held fast, like a paper blown up against a steel mesh fence.

Some years passed, and his father died of a massive coronary, vacationing with his mistress in Baja California.

His mind presents the specter of loss. Life yields this certainty. He has left the tended green of the playing field and got lost among scrub and arroyos. In dreams she appears without words or tears. He has not allowed thoughts of her for over a year. But here she stands inside his tired mind in her completeness.

Colibri.

Inundated now with the glaring daylight world, he sees how his behavior might be viewed as psychotic—the way he threw himself into intimacy with many to mask his grief. Or, maybe it was only greed after all.

After life.

Afterbirth.

Things she hadn't told him. Her dream diaries. She hid them from him. Things he hadn't understood.

He has read documented cases of mental patients with no sense of future or past. Yesterday and tomorrow on either side, like blinders. He doesn't feel real anymore when he is with someone. He has crossed one of those hills we all cross if we get that far. His world has shrunk to just himself.

He knows that space-time cannot be separated from energy-matter. Together they comprise the four corners of our universe. Only in abstraction can they be split apart. Abstract thinking, perhaps, comprises a fifth—with the capacity to interpenetrate the others. He decides that the fewer emotions a person experiences, the more energy-matter he can devote to abstract thought.

He moves to a prime table by the window, seating himself before a tall pane of glass facing the street. Quietly, in the sun, he expresses a social exercise of inner grace. A plump young woman pushing a baby carriage glances his way. She doesn't acknowledge his stare. Most people don't seem to see him now. This must be how it feels when you are old and weak.

He reminds himself to breathe. He always expected to die suddenly. Like his father. Like Colibri. Not this slow disintegration. No children. No brethren. He looks down at his hands.

Rough knuckles splayed out on a flat white surface. Once he wore a watch and ring. Had places to be. People who needed him.

He rises to leave. Fingers confirm the check in his left breast pocket. A bank clerk awaits his monthly transaction. When the anguish threatens to overtake him again, he sees there is this moment only, the moment of decision, orientation, commitment. Turning toward the finest parts of himself, offering up what's left, with dignity and abandon.

Over a period of seven years, David Ambrose Gentry made entries in notebooks under one of three working topics:
    NAMING (how natural forms derive their names)
    S.I.N. (sex in nature)
    RELATIONS (cognition and emotion)

Colibri kept two diaries: one a record of daily life and the other a recurring dream sequence.

All are interspersed here in a roughly chronological manner.

1995 Notebook
David Ambrose

Seahorses mate afloat. The male fertilizes an egg inside the female, while the female injects an egg into the pouch of the male for fertilization. Consequently, both male and female become pregnant. Each remaining pregnant for fifty days. Two new seahorses are spawned—one from each parent. Quite efficient.

Crocodiles: Sex of offspring is entirely determined by temperature of environment where egg was placed.

Vernanimalcula, a creature the size of period at the end of this sentence, was the first proto-sexual organism. Lived in the seas six hundred million years ago. Enlarging reveals complexity. How we found our way to this bi-lateral, sexual path. Monocots dicots pistils stamen. Ovum pollinated.

Darwin's mother was obsessed with the reproductive organs of plant species. Got him started on the birds and bees.

— 3.16.95 S.I.N.

Mom and her beloved Clive asked me to stay another month or two in the house. Instead of moving back to campus, early, as I'd planned. No problem. I enjoy the wooded seclusion—close to the city. You'd never guess, with horses grazing

.e pasture, that we were in the heart of SoCal.

I heard recently that San Diego has more gun stores per capita than any other California metropolis.

Wonder if Mom really cares for the geezer or just needs an escape partner. They've signed up for another cruise, this time aboard the Sea Fever.

The propaganda:

Along with crew and scientists, the Sea Fever accommodates fifteen guests. Fully equipped modern vessel sails the crystal waters of the great Bahamas where schools of dolphins have interacted with humans for centuries. Our agenda involves snorkeling around the Sugar Wreck—a Spanish galleon that went down around 1700—and swimming with the affectionate wild dolphin.

Mating with any consenting adult perhaps?

Testimonial from autistic girl, age seventeen: *Swimming with dolphins was a wonder-dappled interlude between waking and sleeping. . . . When we got back home I felt somehow caught in a dream within the waking state, couldn't tell which is which. And that was so scary, until I realized it's all the same anyhow.*

— 6.2.95 RELATIONS

Diatoms. Smallest living things, next to bacteria and viruses. They accrete as crystal structures of silica, but can also locomote. Plant, animal, neither, or both? Eight thousand species developed twenty-four-million years ago, late Miocene. Same time as early hominids. Asexual lengthwise splitting. A technique reportedly unique in nature.

Due to a flaw in "design" each successive asexual generation tends to get smaller. When they get too small, diatoms, as a species, initiate the sexual process. Which restores them to their original size.

Prolific creatures: "More generations result from a single diatom in one year than all the generations of the human race since it began on earth." No shit.

— 6.11.95 S.I.N.

Visiting Prof, Gerome Sanger, Yale University:
There are important links between the differentiated emotions and the information-processing systems of the human organism. The question is, how can cognition—or information processing—and our emotional response to the information be tied together; and how can we propose theoretical models of how this linkage works. We recognize that people have basic emotions, but there is increasing reason to believe that these emotions emerge in relation to what kind of information exists for us to process.

Huh. I'm more interested in coming at it from the opposite side: How emotions determine

what we experience, what information we "decide" to process.
— 6.19.95 RELATIONS

John last night read to me from his new screenplay based on Wilhelm Reich's "secret life." J. is always a surprise. His curly mop of hair ("carrothead" we used to call him) practically stands on end when he's excited. He's so intense, always moving about, waving his arms. He says Reich believed orgasm occurs in every cell of the body. It's the body's form of electrical balancing—thunderstorm bringing on the rain.

Recently, in Hollywood, J. met Reich's son, who seemed interested in the project. Wants to help sell the thing. Hope that works out for John. He could use a break. A rare bird that guy.

J. stayed over but left shortly before I got up. His half-empty cup of coffee still warm on the counter. Left me some dirty dishes, and a scrawled note: "Back in a few days." No mention of where he was going.

Later in the day, his mom, Anne, came by looking for him. Lingered to chat. She picked up a framed photo from Mom's desk. Impossible shot: J. and I flying high [yeah!] above backyard trampoline.

She'd had it rough. Single mom raising three rowdy sons. I've known her since I started first grade. Met John the first day. I had broken my leg. John was assigned by our teacher to help me get around.

She untied and retied the scarf at her neck, tugged at the hem of her shirt, talked about how disappointed she was that John had given up his research to pursue a writing career. She said how much she *admired me* for "sticking with science."

Admired me. I could hardly believe it. John had always been the star: good-looking, captain of the swim team, writing plays, giving speeches, Thespian Club, that sort of thing. I was the geek, awkward, too tall for my age. Mom called me "a mumbler."

I stood up from behind the desk. Moved closer to Anne, and said, sincerely, "John's always been the creative type. Never had a mind for science." I didn't say that I think he bent his star with too many drugs back in high school.

She looked up at me with a smile, as if waiting, for something.

Of course, I only realized later that she (maybe) wanted to make it with me. If I'd only caught the clues. Can it be true? Holy Mother-of-God-in-Heaven.

— 6.20.95 RELATIONS

How to trace knowledge of plant use through development of nomenclature. Begin with the

Latin/pre-Latin classifications. A plant's uses and purposes [food, remedy, mood amplifier, pain reliever, perfume, or tool: i.e., abortifacient, aphrodisiac, contraception, poison]. Mostly lost to our modern pharmacopoeia. Uses might be retrieved by decoding both Latin derivations and common names.

From course syllabus: *In the nineteenth century, when the origin of language was studied extensively, explanation focused on historical development. Since then, much has been learned about the relationship of language to human biology.*

Need to get my hands on all known classification systems, historic and pre- if possible.

— 6.29.95 NAMING

Simultaneous hermaphroditism [switching during mating] in deep sea fish is due, in part, to the fact that locating a partner can be difficult: *Once thought an oddity, such opportunistic sex changes are more common than previously supposed. Conversions from female to male are known in species from fourteen families. Conversions from male to female found in eight. All species that change their sex have evolved from those whose sex was fixed for life—allowing for greater reproductive success.*

Each fish delivers a few eggs and fertilizes a few.

Switching helps equalize energy demands. It takes *much more* energy to produce eggs than sperm.

One fish says, in effect, to the other, "I'll give you four of my eggs to fertilize if you will give me four of yours." The fish whose turn it is to produce sperm places itself above the other: body cupped to catch the buoyant eggs as they are released.

— 7.7.95 S.I.N.

Weird Names List. People you wonder why the fuck they haven't changed their names:
- Dick Hymen—conducted an all-girl symphony
- Blanche Pughe—director of refuse management
- Most popular girl at Jefferson High—Claudia Pickup
- Class clown—Stu Pidley
- Shirley Bust—junior high slut, bra size 36DDD

Guy on radio last night, named Casio Bowl-a-Puke. At least that's how it sounded. Obviously spelled Beaulepuque or Bollapeuc, or something like that. Singer, Canadian. Plugging his new CD. Good luck to you, buddy!

— 7.12.95 NAMING

From Mom's Soc-Sci newsletter:
In a study done in the late 1980s, Americans rated anger control as one of the most important

personal characteristics. Why, then, are child abuse, domestic violence, and juvenile crime growing exponentially? Is anger now a closet emotion? Don't show it at work. Take it home, or take it out on those who won't fight back. . . .

Got me thinking about Dad. Polite and functioning most of the time. But when he drank, especially at night, he almost always grew angry. And violent. I never knew where the anger came from. He managed to be in control at work—CEO of top-level investment company. Mom generally protected me from his outbursts. But one time—I was five or six—I came into their bedroom and saw him pelting her with razor blades.

She stood there crying. Arms at her sides.

I ran at him shrieking. Punched him repeatedly in the gut.

She kicked him out when I was nine. I remember her crying a lot at dinner. He phoned late at night, sent threatening letters. Eventually, agreed to a divorce and she got this house and the land.

Mom believed it was genetic. Said that Dad's father had been an extremely brutal man. One time, annoyed that his sons had disobeyed him, he made them watch as he took the newborn kittens out of the litter box and hurled them at the wall, one by one.

These are not good characteristics to inherit. Genetic or retroactively compensatory? My first girlfriend, Donna, called me a "dumb fuck jerk ass monster." We broke up. [I had started going out with Ellen and hadn't thought to clue in Donna.] I used to slam doors and hang up on Do. I used to have tantrums, Mom tells me. Her side of the family is different. More sane. She said that at first she believed she could change Dad. She perceived that he was damaged. But felt her love for him was strong enough. Sad ending. He died suddenly. No reconciliation.

— 7.13.95 RELATIONS

Mom leased to NARHA—North American Riding for the Handicapped Association—two of our older horses for therapeutic uses. People who cannot walk normally find riding a cantering horse the closest they can come to natural walking. Stimulation to the hips, spine, nerves, and muscles. Which in turn affects the entire body and clears the mind. Positive impact on the neurological system too. Improvements in balance, coordination, fine motor skills, emotional stability, and speech. Mom explains, "Horses are motivators. Self-esteem is increased when a person learns to control an animal that may outweigh her by 1200 pounds."

Mom currently defines herself as a "relationship scientist." A misnomer, I think, because she concentrates intensely on one individual at a time—although in relation to a group, such as family or co-workers. She's writing a paper about the effect of cultural "swarm patterns" on the individual. Says we see them all the time in fashion, education, consumerism, slang, technology, and spiritual fads.

She and Clive are in New York City, now working with Korean immigrant youths. She was asked to speak before The Council on Competitiveness in Washington DC. Go Mom!

Leaving Dad was the best thing that happened to her. Clive is another story. One of those aging hippie poet types. Halo of white hair. Bills himself as a "picture-reader." Says he can tell what's wrong with you by looking at your photograph. He actually sits around a lot watching big screen TV. Wears headphones so as not to disturb anyone. Clive says that the molecular and atomic makeup of the emulsion resonates at the identical frequency of the objects it represents. What say? Photo-homeopathy?

Clive's okay. Treats me fine. And Mom seems to genuinely enjoy being with him. That's the important thing.

Got the whole place to myself for four weeks. Then, back to school. And, if all works out as planned, three months in Mexico, praying that my Scripps fellowship comes through. Grunt work, really, at a miniscule marine bio center.

That's fine with me. I turn twenty-one tomorrow. Think I'll throw myself a little party. Haven't done much socializing lately.
— 8.24.95 RELATIONS

I'm into the Gauloises: gall, Gaul, gaol? Nasty things. Don't really enjoy drinking or drugs all that much but recently took up smoking. Mostly do it at home when I'm alone. Names of the brands intrigue me: Marlboro, Thins, Viceroy, Kool, Kent, Spirit, Camel, Carlton, Pall Mall, Doral, Vantage, Parliament, Tareyton, Benson & Hedges, Lucky Strike, Salem, Winston. What's the difference? Names designed to appeal to vanity. Various personality profiles. I'll quit after I've tried them all.

Tobacco's a New World native, revered for medicinal and stimulative properties. What were the French smoking before Columbus sailed?
— 8.30.95 NAMING

Aside from alcoholism in my biological father and paternal grandfather (the Sicilian) I appear to have inherited longevity genes. Dad died in his late-fifties but most of his family survived past a hundred.

The men on my mother's side, Irish and English, have lived into their nineties. And the women are vigorous producers of offspring.

Mom only had me. Don't think I'll marry. I'll die before my time without any children. Back to

the grind next week. Feeling kind of low today.
— 9.1.95 RELATIONS

SF Institute publication: *. . . if the individual is skilled at grappling with its environment, it will survive to the age of reproduction, and successfully produce offspring. A digital entity, too, must have the ability to reproduce itself. First there needs to be an entire population of self-reproducing digital entities, and there must be variety within the population.*

Sex among self-replicating, constantly evolving digital entities?

Sex among proto-life strings of amino acid complexes?

I told Mom what I was reading, because she asked.

She laughed. She thinks I'm a bonehead. Tells me I'm too skinny. Need to get more sun. Standing behind me, at my desk, messing up my hair. She knows I hate that. She says, "David, dear, women know that love and sex are not the same thing. I think you may be a little unusual in that you are twenty-one years old, you're intelligent, sensitive, and attractive [at least *she* thinks so], yet you've never been in love. No one has captured your heart. When you fall, you will fall very hard."
— 9.5.95 S.I.N.

Bats are of the order Chiroptera, "winged hand." Example of how form and function are incorporated into a name. Dig: a bat eats the fruit then flies over a barren region and drops seed with its feces. Bat droppings amount to the largest percentage of natural seed plantings in devastated areas. Creating new ecosystems. Bat mothers often altruistically feed non-kin. The "winged hand" produces *mucho guano*. Major source of fertilizer in underdeveloped countries. It says here that studying bats led to the development of navigational devices for the blind, and of course radar. Helping hands.
— 10.13.95 NAMING

Oaxaca, Mexico: Got my stint at Scripps in neurobiology, specifically: "The role of serotonin on dominance-aggression signaling in crustaceans." How's that for a topic? Will be collecting data at a remote marine reserve near Puerto Angel, several hours drive from Oaxaca. Had been hoping for assignment near one of those elite resort towns where all the hot young babes are bored stiff (or loose) vacationing with parents. Not my fate.

    Flew into the *aeropuerto* yesterday. Spending a couple of days in town before hooking up with co-worker, Jack, who drives us to the Center.

    This is such a beautiful city. Greenery, clean streets, stately nineteenth-century buildings. The young women are gorgeous but dignified. Even the older ones have an appealing grace. The pace of life is slower here. European-style bakeries. Great coffee, warm and chocolaty. People strolling, riding bikes with stacks of warm tortillas in their baskets.

Big surprise today. I met an amazing girl. I watched her from across the street, she was standing outside the Del Palacio Museum, waiting for the autobús. I was struck by the way she held herself. Poised and steady. Modestly dressed. Dark hair pulled back neatly. I wondered if I could ever have such a creature in my life.

I crossed the street to get a closer look, and as I passed by her, she turned and asked, "Por favor, Señor, what is the hour?," tapping her bare wrist.

I was astonished that she spoke to me: a foreigner and a stranger.

I told her the time. It was half past two. She introduced herself as María Cuerno y Saeta.

"You can call me Colibri."

She wrote it down for me, on a page torn from a small spiral notebook she took from her pocket. "No accent," she said. She's a real cutie. Bright, sweet, too young I'm sure. I asked if she had time to show me some sights, as I had only just arrived. She nodded, adjusted her canvas satchel—full of books, I noticed—and gestured toward the Zócalo. Town's leafy central square.

We sat on a bench and I detected a delicious scent, like vanilla or lemon mixed with chocolate. Not sure if it came from her or the enormous trumpet-shaped flowers hanging overhead.

I told her about my fellowship as a researcher. That I was interested in the names of the local flora.

She paused along the path to point out a few exotic species. A boy ran by dressed as a skeleton. In preparation for some festivity, I guessed. She laughed and said something to him in Spanish, which I didn't catch.

In English, Spanish, some Latin, she named various species for me. The Latin, she said, she learned from her grandmother, who had sadly "passed on."

Odd variety of pear tree bearing enormous globose fruit. Huge bald cypresses sporting air-rooted epiphytes. Enormous Cereus sending their "organ pipes" skyward. Fantastic hairy cactuses I've seen only in botanical gardens. A paradise.

Colibri said she's more familiar with the names and uses for the *plantas* in her area. Nueva Villa Flores. About ninety kilometers from here.

Can't seem to find it on my map.

We paused in front of the Catedral de Santo Domingo where young people gather along the high adobe walls. Talking, holding hands, laughing, lightly caressing.

Girls here go barefoot or wear high heels.

Tight, revealing clothing. No cleavage, but a lot of make-up. Pendants on chains bearing images of saints.

I've been to Oaxaca before. Brief stay, many years ago with Dad. Don't remember seeing anything like this.

Colibri was wearing a dark skirt and a white stitched blouse fastened at the neck with colored ribbons. Rope sandals. Pale shiny toenails against her tawny skin.

I foolishly made a move to take her hand, when she suddenly raised her arm and shouted, "Raúl!"

I saw a thick, rangy, military-type heading our way.

"*Mi hermano*," she said quickly. "I've got to go."

She promised to meet me again, in two weeks. Same place same time. Beautiful dark sensuous eyes. Is this a dream? Am I imagining things?

I pray that the hulk is truly her brother and not my competition.

+++

Trying now to nab some supplemental research funds. Colibri could be a help to us. To me, particularly. In my nascent, esoteric field of research: the encoding of chemical properties of botanicals. Naming. Nomenclature.

Here for just six weeks, returning spring.
In Spanish, Colibri means "hummingbird."
The guidebook says: *Hummingbirds fly in large figure eights. Heart beats 260 times per second. Each bird eats half its body weight a day . . . most mate only once in life.*
— 12.12.95 NAMING

From current research:
The behavior of an individual organism is regulated by the organism's internal and external environments. Many central questions in the field of neuroscience are concerned with how this regulation is brought about. The presence of other individuals, the perception of reduction in survival resources, or competition for access to mates are all examples of situations that provoke specific responses.

An explicit contrast can be drawn between "costly signaling,"—i.e., a male peacock's extravagant display or the color coding of crab claws—and the "cheap" signals employed in linguistic communication. A phrase such as, "Hey baby let's dance," is cheaper to manage than a display of complex evolutionary signal development.

I know I need to see Colibri again. How does she figure in the equation?
— 12.15.95 RELATIONS

1996 Notebooks: David Ambrose Gentry

Back at University:

Does the word carve out new pathways or do the pathways come first. Edelstein's view derives from his work in immunology. Determining how the immune system learns to recognize and imitate an invader.

"Take the Shakespearean sonnet," he says. "The brain learns to recognize a form and then it can imitate and improve on the form. That's how variations occur. Similar to antigen receptivity."

I disagree. There is much more to sending and receiving a "message" in poetry than retrofitted recognition. Talk to John about this. He's got a lot to say about words.

My research needs narrowing and focus. Must be clearly identified by end of next year. Return to Oaxaca in June. Plans that involve Colibri.

Focus on relationship of language to biology? Investigate the adaptation of language as a stimulant and mood elevator? How language might itself create neurological anomalies.

Take the word "fuck." It has been shown to produce a measurable rise in feelings of anger, gaiety, and / or sexual arousal. If overused as a stimulant, emotional response declines.

— 3.14.96 NAMING

Notes for overdue Cog. Sci. paper:
Perception of linear time is a peculiarly human emotion. Why do we have the feeling that time is a continuum? Is it because our physically limited methods of processing are, in essence, eschatological, moving toward an end? One's own death is the "end-product" of life.

Since the Enlightenment, information has been organized along lines of logical progression. The scroll, the book, lines of type on a screen. Time as a continuous unfolding may be one of our grand cultural delusions.

It has been proposed that within any so-called "moment" a person has about thirty seconds of total eidetic recall, in which one can go backward or forward in time.

Digital/electronic time pieces are based on, and measure, pulsations in matter. Contracting or expanding a piece of quartz by placing it between two metal plates provokes a flow of electrons toward one of the surfaces, causing microscopic vibrations which can be translated into mechanical oscillations. The precise regularity of these oscillations is a function of the almost perfect crystalline structure of the quartz. However, the high precision of a quartz clock lasts only a few years. Crystals age, as do all aggregates of matter.

Our sense of time is connected with apprehension of the flux and flow of information from our environment. Internal and external. Perception, sensation, and emotion are all engaged. Why aren't time pieces based on bodily calibrations, such as, the pulse, the breath, the firing of neuro-transmitters? Because those calibrations are extremely unstable and variable *within any agreed-upon time.*

"Every indivisible moment of duration is everywhere, " wrote Newton (*Principia*, 1687). It was with the application of mathematics that the Newtonian concept of time became a glorified straight line. A line going in one direction only and never intersecting itself. Such a perception of time gives poignancy to life, intensifying our awareness of the inevitability of death.

Aside: Sir Isaac Newton, the great mind, produced no offspring that anybody knows about. Was that practical efficiency or a waste of superfine genetic code? Need more biographical information.

Memory is a key to unlocking our own and our collective cellular history. But "memory" is only part of our memories. Much of memory comes directly from the imagination. And much of memory contributes to any singular perception of "the moment."

In Newton's concept, time is continuous. Two instants—however close together—contain intermediate instants that each contain the "present instant." According to Newton, the fact that any present instant can retrace its steps, makes it, in a sense, *reversible.* He believed that evolution and history could, strictly speaking, reverse directions.

Stephen Hawking came at it later after much fussing with quantum physics.

Heisenberg's *minimal interval* is a second divided by a number equal to one followed by 26 zeros. His theory states that there are more of those intervals in one second than there have been seconds since the formation of the earth.

— 10:47 pm 4.18.96 RELATIONS

Earlier today I watched a yellow spider. Crawling on the wall above my desk. Shiny black tips on hairy yellow legs. Now I see the same spider curled up beneath my lamp. Dead apparently. The time when I observed it alive on the wall seems to have occurred *before* this time of contemplation. The death of the spider appears irreversible. However, it *is* reversible *in my mind,* which is what I was, in fact doing just now by picturing the spider while writing these words. Re-reading what I just said does the same thing.

Note: smoked the excellent weed/tobacco blend John dropped off this morning.

— 2:00 am 4.18.96 RELATIONS

This summer, if all goes as I planned, Colibri and I will return together, to spend two months here at the house while Mom and Clive go whale watching with a tagging crew ship.

Colibri and I have been communicating through post cards. She sends pictures of flowers and I send ones of horses.

C. is hesitant to consider my "proposal." However, we have developed a strong bond. I think I can talk her into it. I think I can make her trust me. She's a very bright girl and needs to see more of the world.

C. told me she believes "the names of things" were given to us by God, as it says in The Bible. But she doesn't accept the Adam and Eve part of the story. She says Eve received the names of things from the serpent. God's only competition. Eve was named "keeper of the names." God got wind of it and kicked them out on their butts. Adam then had to learn the names from her, in order to survive.

Colibri explained that in Spanish the father's surname is followed by the mother's maiden name. However a person is addressed by the father's surname not by the mother's. Colbri's given name is María Cuerno y Saeta.

Cuerno, m., Spanish, huntsman's horn, crescent moon.

Saeta, f., Latin, arrow, dart, hand of a clock.

If widowed, Spanish women usually abandon their husband's name but the children have the choice to use either. This custom apparently dates back to ancient Rome.

Once the divorce was final, Mom asked me to agree to have our names legally changed to her mother's maiden name, Gentry. I was born a Scalpino. We don't mention them anymore.

Finally ready. Packed my bags. Tomorrow I return to Mexico.

— 5:45 am 6.16.96 NAMING

Oaxaca:
I stumble on a festival in full swing, sensory feast of Corpus Christi. The whole town bursting with revelry. Strings of electric bulbs crisscrossing cobbled streets. A band of strolling musicians, sleek in black/red suits. Wild dancing *abuelitos* wearing bright green devil masks. Enormous clown feet. Baseball caps studded with flowers. Chinese umbrella hats dangling rabbit's feet. Diesel fumes and dayglow fruit. Sweet milky liquor shared with skateboarders and prostitutes . . . makes me drunk at once. Man dressed as nun hands out small packets with instructions: *Como Usar un Condón.* Sulfur smell of fireworks. Warm tortillas fried in lard. Roasted prickly pear washed down with shots of *mezcal.* Booted *campesinos* arm-in-arm with green-haired punks and gangly

high-heeled *travestidos*. Courtyard of the Basílica de Soledad alive with *música folklórica*. Stadium speakers blasting distortion from makeshift stage. State Police cruise in steel blue sedans. On back of a flat-bed truck, *guardia* wield M-16s. Gang of toughs in army caps emblazoned with "GS" logo. What does that stand for?

I napped in a fine mist under the "monkey hand" tree. Waxy aromatic petals with red claw-like stamens. Revered for its healing properties.

Strange dream. Calm morning. Few signs of last night's merriment. Straw angels fluttering in the breeze. Dragged myself to the bus station. Instructions in hand. Colibri insisted I take First Class which has windows with coverings "to draw against the heat."

— 6.17.96 RELATIONS

Oaxaca dream:
The Doctor. Recurring dream character. Far distant future. He's traveled to Africa to find the only remaining natural land formation. Everything has been built upon everything else. The ground is covered over by the products of civilization. Underground levels and high-rises span the planet.

Doctor asks a khaki-shirted worker where he might find the "natural land form." Pointing, glaze-eyed, the man states: "Walk all the way to the end of the mall. You can view it through the glass." This is a mall I recognize—a newly built monstrosity across from Scripps on Torrey Pines Road. Finding an exit, Doctor moves into open sky. Crosses an enormous paved area, cracked and patched with tar. Ahead, the shape of a rugged mass of dirt, rocks, trees. Plot of wilderness at the whim of sun and rain.

The thought of such freedom, such randomness, makes him tremble. Arouses his lust. Closing in, he sees the ground is made of clods of dirt, half-burnt, alive with worms. Rock ledges fracture and crumble into dust. Hills covered with grasses and dead leaves seethe in decay.

A fecund scent of birth, feces, mating.

He clutches the steel fence. Feeling the pull of what's inside. The ground swarms with ants. Large red ants, small sleek black ones, pale ones with transparent wings. Hurriedly working, fighting, carrying food. Removing dead things.

The area is protected by miles of chain link topped with coils of razor wire. Steel spikes secure the bottom. Somehow he must vault the fence to reach the soft earth.

— 6.17.96 S.I.N.

Colibri and I sit on a ledge overlooking a narrow rocky beach near Puerto Escondido. Forty KM on rough road from her village. Just up the coast from my little live-in marine lab. Overcast sky.

The sea alive. Wildly in motion.

Colibri watches seagulls "flirt with the waves."

Check this, I say. Reading aloud from a recent SFI newsletter:

Self-replicating creatures in a fixed soup would soon fill the soup and lock up the system. It's necessary, then, to program in a "reaper." Creatures can be killed by de-allocating their memory and removing them from the mix. However, each individual's dead cell code is retained in the soup.

She laughs, shaking her finger at me:

"What is wrong with you men? . . . programming in a reaper!"

She is so lively. Lovely. I ache when I look at her. Must be patient.

Mostly busywork for Jack and me. Easy to complete each day's task in an hour. I spend every available moment with Colibri. Jack is glum when I rush off to see her. Nothing for him to do. Wants to play pool. [Made the mistake of telling him Colibri is a hotshot player.]

I don't want to share her with him. Or with anyone. Taking it slow. Afraid I will ruin everything. Trying desperately to keep it platonic [for now], me and C.

Concerns about her safety. Her goddam future for chrissake. I'm in way over my head. She's alone most of the time on that worthless plot

of land. Her brother's gone a lot. There's some tragic family history which she's only hinted at. Daily I'm offering irresistible arguments for her to come back with me for the months Mom and Clive will be away.
— 6.26.96 RELATIONS

The Return: Colibri and I camped last night on the shores of the blue-black lake. Southern tip of New Mexico. Artesia. Named after a place in France with natural up-thrusting waters. Reddish dust and heat. Sense of endless possibility. . . .

A human being, writes Monroe, *is incapable of experiencing a strong physical stimulus without attaching a deeper meaning to it.* His writing has been a guide these past few months. Difficult decisions.

I couldn't keep my promise to myself. We made love on C's birthday. She turned eighteen. It was the most amazing thing I've ever experienced. She said she wouldn't come north with me unless she found out if we were *"con buena amistad."* She's way too wise for her age.

Our route: We flew out of Oaxaca, changed planes in Mexico City, and landed in Torreón. There I purchased "Hondo," as we named him. Our bright green, '68 Ford, half-ton truck. Taking the long route out of Juárez, skirting the lip of Texas, we've come up through Carlsbad.

Following the old highways.

Drove through the day and into the night. Crossed the border at El Paso. Told the border guards Colibri was my "fiancée." She showed her passport and work permit. The crossing was surprisingly easy. I had all the paperwork ready about work and airplane tickets. They seemed most concerned about the truck. One guard blatantly flirted with Colibri. She was cool. Even though they did go through her purse after thoroughly scouring the truck cab. Looking for drugs I suppose.

Didn't find the bag of flowers and seeds she'd hidden in her lace up boots. Her coolness comes in handy. Those are her special flowers, she says. Ones she uses to alleviate the pains, her "dolores."

Science was about the creation of metaphor back in the days of Aristotle. Newton emphasized empiricism. Measuring, accumulating facts. But clearly, abstract thinking includes the mythic. Colibri says the Zapotec believed the natural world had a supernatural counterpart. Parallel to or inside this one. There are slits you can peer through. Pass through physically at times, she says.

C. notes the names of RV's we pass: Companion, Command, Explorer, Ventura, Sidekick, Fireball, Mohave, Warrior, Pting!, Prowler, Silver Streak, Argosy, Lazy-Daze . . . We stop often and walk into the brush. She points out the plants that are similar to ones in her part of Mexico. Grasses, cactuses, yucca, cottonwoods, screw-bean mesquite, piñon, ocotillo.

"Mis hermanitas," she calls them, "my little sisters."

I believe everything she says.

Can't imagine living a minute without her.

How did this happen to me?

Jimson weed in bloom with its enormous cream-white trumpet flowers. Tobacco-scented leaves. C. calls it "sagrada datura." Her grandmother told her it's a powerful protector of mankind. "Likes to eat up devils." Hence it's known as the devil weed.

I always thought the "devil" part referred to its psychotropic properties. Unpredictable in the extreme.

I suggested we crush a few seeds and eat them. Colibri warned that the only way to use this plant is to let its *potencia* seep into your skin. She placed a leaf inside her bra. Had me put a few into my sock. Later, I saw her stash some leaves and flowers into a little pillow she'd brought along.

"First," she said smiling slyly, "you make friends with it. Then you seduce it into leaning you its power." Loaning, lending, she means? Leaning. I like that.

Hwy. 285 out of Artesia, 380 West past El Capitan. We discuss mining. C. doesn't believe in removing things from inside the earth. Says that metals and chemicals can be retrieved gently off the surface using simpler techniques.

I explain that civilization would not exist without mining. We wouldn't be riding in this fine green four-speed half-ton truck just now without the mining of metals and petroleum. And the airplane we will board for San Diego:

"You want it to be made of cardboard and tree sap?"

That made her laugh. She laughed and laughed, almost hysterically, her thick dark hair falling in waves across her face. Then, abruptly, knotting her hair over one shoulder, she stared straight ahead in that way she has of keeping still.

I barely perceived her eyelashes flicker from the effort at self-control.

At times, in her stoicism, I see the *indígena* in her . . . Mixtec, Mayan? Her heritage is confused. (Whose isn't?) She's confused. She's courageous. I know that. Agreeing to come with me was hard for her.

The old truck died in Socorro. We abandoned it outside the cathedral. Note inside the windshield, "FREE TRUCK, KEYS IN IGNITION."

Just around the corner from . . . guess what?

The New Mexico Institute of Mining and Technology.

— 7.3.96 NAMING

Socorro thankfully had a small airport. Nice old guy gave us a lift in his personal red and white twin-engine Cesna. All the way to Albuquerque. Time to kill before the flight to San Diego. Got some coffee, bought a local paper, found our way to an overlook of the mighty muddy Rio Grande. Discovered this article, confirming what C. had recently explained:

WEED CONSUMES PLUTONIUM

Hallucinogenic jimson weed, also called Datura, will soon be used to "eat plutonium" as part of new environmental cleanup technology.

Biochemist Paul Jackson of Los Alamos National Laboratory has identified toxic waste isolation properties in the weed and found it effective in the filtering of plutonium-contaminated water, according to LANL spokesman, James Gustafson.

"Jimson weed cells don't actually 'eat' the plutonium," Gustafson said, referring to the catch-phrase for the waste-isolation process. He explained that scientists at the Lab had built filters made from jimson-weed cells, which are much easier to handle and dispose of than radioactive water. Cells from the plant can also decompose highly-explosive materials, along with the 'pink water' waste from the manufacturing process. Gustafson said that scientists working with Jackson have patented the new filter . . .

C. told me of another plant her grandmother introduced her to. Known as "leaves of Mary the Shepherdess," or *Salvia divinorum*, a perennial mint native to Sierra Mazateca region of Oaxaca. She said it's powerful for visions. To be used only after fasting and prayers to Mother Mary. And only in times of dire confusion.

"Questions asked with sincerity will be answered . . ."

She described the plant in detail. Leaf shape, when it flowers, where to find it. The best method for ingestion seems to be to chew a few previously masticated leaves. Here's the kicker: premastication is best done by a celibate nun.

Does she make up this stuff?

I don't think so. I haven't met a more conscientious person than Colibri. She could be doing the most simple things, and I see tremendous beauty in her actions.

"David, why are you to become a scientist?"

"Uh, I guess I'm drawn to the factual. Nobody's going to give me a paycheck for dealing with the incommensurable."

"Why are you taking me to California? You are sure you know what you are doing? Your parents will not like me. What will your friends say? You are foolish like that flower, *impatiens,* the one that when you touch, it explodes flinging all its seeds far and away." — 7.4.96 NAMING

Colibri has been to the U.S. before. To visit her sister in Texas. That sister later died in some kind of accident. Haven't yet pressed for details.

She's got nobody except that bum of a brother, Raúl.

On the Southwest flight, C. doesn't want to sit by the window. Says she's seen enough of clouds.

Nearing San Diego, I notice her discomfort as the plane circles and circles, awaiting landing clearance.

"Don't worry," I say, "this isn't deep water, only the bay."

To distract her, I begin telling her last night's dream about the ocean. More of my fucking negativity. Partway into it I realize this was no ordinary dream but a nightmare vision. Was it the devil weed seeping into my bloodstream?

Fortunately, at that moment, the plane tilts steeply to descend. Engine roars, she grasps my arm, closes her eyes. Singing a little tune. One I recognize.

Do you love me as I love you? Will you change my life, or will this dream of mine fade out of sight . . . like the moon growing dim . . .

I'm hoping she's forgotten the grim tale I began. Once we're in the Airporter to take us to the city, she looks me straight in the eye and says with excruciating calm:

"I have dreams about the ocean too. Tell me the rest of yours."

Last night's dream:

. . . At my back, miles to the north, the city. All around, pale rocks, dry dirt. The brick-like soil is cracked. Thick brittle chips litter a lake-sized area off to my right. Chalcocite. Scrappy bushes cling to the edges of ravines. It hasn't rained for a very long time.

The sorry-looking sheep stands at my side. No ordinary sheep, this one is nearly a phantom. Almost entirely made of trash. The kind found under an overpass. Or in back-street gutters.

The sheep nibbles a dried-out clump of bunch-grass. Its neck bends and I observe ragged strips of flesh separating from the papery bones. This sheep is in the final stages of degeneration. Approximately four feet high, its entire body weight can't possibly exceed five pounds.

The sheep gives off no odor. Neither do the other animals who've contracted this unnamable disease. The lack of scent is one of the clearest warning signs. Living things are composed of aromatic substances. Carbon-based molecules arranged in benzene rings. These animals don't rot. They cannot metabolize, reproduce, or repair themselves. They cannot even die without our help. . . .

As the animals disintegrate, fragments of host cells are borne on the wind. Infecting others. Plant life, too, has been affected. Down to the simplest of mosses and lichen. The disease agent doesn't need light. It remains dormant in the recesses of matter.

This particular animal has been "a guide" for some time. Leading me and Jack to the hiding places. Tattered streamers of pelt flail out behind as it trots heedlessly off to the next outcropping.

You would not immediately recognize this creature as a sheep. You might not be able to "see" it at all, if you encountered it when it was standing still.

I know what it is because it is my job to know.

Once I cured ordinary diseases of animals and human beings. My tools were my hands, needles, scalpels, chemicals, and radiology. My mental apparatus was aligned along an axis of concern.

My job now is to locate and eradicate all carriers of the disease. Of all sexes and species. We've been tracking this area for six weeks. Jack comes up carrying our gear. We've arrived at another den. Teeming with the ailing creatures.

As soon as they expose themselves, whether to flee or plea for help, Jack shoots them. His aim is excellent. The creatures are dead while they dream. We impale their carcasses on galvanized hooks. Drag them off to an arroyo where thousands at a time lie exposed to the stingy winter sun.

I glance at the sun. I can stare at it here.

Filtered through infinitesimal particles pervading the atmosphere. I'm disturbed by the noise that escapes the conflated bellies of the animals as the shatter bullets pierce their hides. A high-pitched whine. Raspy edges.

It's my duty to ignore sensations and feelings. Immunity depends on allowing no emotive repercussions. If an emotion begins to arise, perhaps generated by thoughts or memory, I must instantly dispel it. Or I too will fall ill.

We throw the entities into the ditch. Some were once camels, elephants, coyotes, cougars, giraffes. They retain so little mass when reduced by this insidious disease it is impossible to identify them.

Dust thickens. The breeze contracts. Jack has reloaded. He's taking aim again. This time at a large black beetle about a yard off to the right. Scalloped tracks winding off into the distance. This beetle has traveled an arduous path.

"Let it go." I caution. Noticing the dense and glossy carapace.

Jack nods. Re-sheathes his gun. And extracts a roll of 3mm opaque plastic sheeting.

"What about him?"

He gestures toward the sheep who hovers at the edge of the ditch, staring down into it.

"How long ya gonna let that one go?"

Jack has little patience. Even less sense most

of the time. But now he's right. It's time. My turn to fire.

I remove my gun from its protective bladder, enjoying the sensation of its heft and gleam. Emptying my mind, my fingers find the proper engagement.

I reconsider... watching the sheep's absurdly playful gambol toward me. Harrowing devotion without reason. Soon he will know his enemy. ... Each night he sleeps outside the cocoon's entrance slit. When we emerge at dawn, he jumps up and runs in large concentric circles. The basal ganglia are early affected. Restrictive damage induces persistent circling in mammals. And a hypertrophic condition known as "obstinate progression."

Hesitation is overcome by reminding myself that this creature is nothing but air. A half-formed idea about things that once were.

Begin again. Everything sucked back into the viscous opening. To be reconnoitered, revised, spit back out again.

Thinking now of the canal sal se puedes *in Baja Gulf where I vacationed once with a lovely woman. Eons ago. Volumes of water are sucked down at the north and sides, moving rapidly southward at the bottom. Everything on the bottom, except the largest boulders, is swept away. And at the south end of the channel it all shoots high up into the air, cascading back onto the calm turquoise waters. Astounding.*

I remind myself that for these long weeks of labor we have come no closer to the source.

Leveling my gun, I fire. Pinning the sheep squarely in the mouth. He stands looking at me for a moment. Then collapses. Jack throws one more deflated form into the ditch. We complete our chores by covering the entire depression end-to-end with plastic. Sealing it off with large rocks. A crew will arrive by heli to incinerate. Even so, the threat persists. The area must be cordoned off for millennia.

We move on. . . .

The resort, I'm told, houses two horses who may be communicators. It looks like the kind of place that serves bad men good beer. I locate the manager. He seems unnecessarily friendly at first. Then, upon questioning becomes fiercely recalcitrant.

Doesn't he know this is for the good of us all?

"You cannot go into the rooms nor the garages without my permission and I shan't give it you."

Where does he get this archaic petulance? I notice a dull film over one of his eyes. For an instant I feel compassion. Retrogressive, hemispherical dominance. He's soon to be dead too.

"Thank you, Sir." I fake politeness to gain

precious moments. We will return at night. A task I dread. I cross the boardwalk to where Jack rests against the railing, picking green paint off the head of a nail.

The railing is green, the eaves are green, the awnings match. All the trim has been recently painted a glossy garish green.

Is this an attempt to prevent our impending discovery?

My thinking seems foggy. I know I'm tired. I hope that's all it is.

Suddenly it becomes clear to me that I'm afraid of when or where or how the moment will present itself. The moment I am called upon to do what I have to do. Will I be able to recall the precise wording of the instructions? Will I stand up to the test?

No one in sight. Jack has wandered off. I'm alone at the railing.

Across the yellow grass, beyond the ridge of granite boulders, out past the abandoned mica mines, there is the sea. I detect its living force moving in on the wind from the west. The wild-looking sky warns of chubasco. *Winds of hurricane force rushing up from the south.*

But look, the sea, endless as weight.

Look, the sea, waiting endlessly. . . .

The scent of the sea restores my balance and sense of purpose. Way out, pulsing and swaying in motion, the molten sea brims with thalassia grasses, blood-red algae, liver-colored kelp, purple belolo eels, olive ridley and aged tortuga turtles, sunfish and kingfish and pan-eyed flounder, the blue-moon jellyfish, the striped big-mouth bass, plankton and shrimp, the magnificent manta ray, finback whales and sailfish, sweet-flavored butter clams, the short-finned pilot whales, the manatee, shark, and leatherfin, the spotted sand bass, flag cabrilla, berrugato croakers and calyfin corvina, the slow-moving vieja fish, the wahoo, the black marlin. . .

Whatever stays in the sea, I know, will have a better chance of it.

— 7.6.96 NAMING

DIARY:
Colibri, Mexico 1992-1996

December 17, 1992
Dearest Diary: Today I take up this pen to tell you about myself and to offer you my thoughts and feelings.

I write in my second tongue, English, so that Raúl, mi hermano, should he ever stumble across these words, will not be able to enter them into his meaning.

I feel so alone. I need someone to hear my secrets.

I am fourteen-and-a-half years old, Mi Diario. Colibri is the name I have chosen for myself. It names the tiny bird that flits from flower to flower with speed and skill. Never stationary, its wings in motion make a blur of color. Though it is the smallest bird in the world, Colibri is "pugnacious" (it says in a book from mi madre). It feeds mostly on flower nectar but will also eat aphids, insects, and spiders when necessary, preferring the arid slopes and the flowering agave from Chisos to the Chiapas. This tiny creature is to be my inspiración.

February 1993
Dear Diario:
My brother, Raúl, exploded into drink again today. Como siempre. It is Sunday. After morning target

practice, he bought a bottle of distillate with our last pesos (he is not aware that I have stashed quite many away). I had asked him to bring home flour and butter, and this is what he did instead. . . .

One wave of a petty war washed over this sorry village leaving in its wake torturers, tourists, addicts, and derelicts. Raúl is of the later persuasion, commonly referred to as a "drake" after the famous English explorer and plunderer.

Nueva Villa Flores, as it's named by some, lies inland from the coast, fifty kilometers or so by dirt track from Puerto Escondido (they have a small aeropuerto). We sit on a wide plateau bordered by the converging of three rivers, Río Verde, Río Atoyac, and Río Yolótepec, under the gaze of the lofty Sierra de Miahuatlán with pine startled peaks.

Father's family engaged in the noble occupation of farming. Unlike most of our neighbors, we still own our land. The soil es muy fecundo but Raúl has not let his fingers touch a plow for years. I ask him to save money for purchase of a tractor. I will drive it myself. I want to work the earth. Raúl has lost sight of the power of the living verde. He sees only Yankee green.

My Grandma (his also, sad to say) told me that anything you can put a price on doesn't have real value.

Raúl has put a cheap price on his soul.

It is just me and him since the time when our parents perished while visiting Grandma in the state of Chiapas. Grandma was a devout Catholic of Mayan descent. She was not killed in that conflagration, but she died too, some years later, under a cloud of mystery. At the age of nine I became an orphan. Some months later, my older hermana, sweet sister Ysabel, passed away after her car was struck by a drunk driver as she traveled the river route returning to her husband in Quemado, Texas, U.S.A.

She had come back home to take care of the legalities. She wanted me to come back with her, to the United States, but I was afraid of so much change so fast. Grandma and the twins would see to my upbringing, they assured her. Raúl, too, was con amistad back then.

Ysabel had always been my closest ally. How different my life would be now, were she still living.

The twins—my eldest brother and sister—may be alive, no one knows where. Twenty years my senior, they are progeny of Mama's first marriage. I barely remember them. They ran away together the summer the borrachos took over our vicinity. Many of my uncles and aunts have died, one way or another. I have some cousins somewhere, and a few school friends, and my teachers in Oaxaca. But that leaves the two of us here, alone, in the world. Me and Raúl.

We own this land, for whatever good it can do us. The government didn't give it to us. It has been owned and worked by mi familia for two centuries. Corn won't turn a profit anymore. Most towns buy from the government-owned haciendas, or they purchase U.S. import. Raúl wants to grow marijuana. I say cacao or coffee or hierbas medicinales, and beans and melón. He's too lazy to do anything.

"Raúl, you bum," I whisper, letting my lips brush his ear. He sleeps on the sofa, with his bad eye open, under the portrait of a dark-haired reclining lady who plays with her pearls. I imagine her dreaming of the land she came from. An island in the Mediterranean. . . .

She was painted on canvas in the nineteenth century. My mother brought her to this house before I was born. (Some say it is a portrait of Mama, in her younger days. A memento of her former life in Mexico City with her wealthy vaquero husband, who died in a mysterious fire.)

Father was kind enough to take pity on a "used woman." She came to live with him on this hilly farm with her expensive dresses and her oil paintings and her calfskin-covered books. She taught me English as soon as I could speak. She arrived as a young woman in Mexico after the Second World War, born in France, of Jewish faith. She studied at fine schools and learned her Spanish in Spain. Even so, she was extraño to the villagers. As she was not of Catholic faith, many looked down on her. I was born in 1978, when she was forty-seven years old. My dearly departed sister, my brother Raúl, and I share the same father.

Papá was slender with a strong mustache. He carved animals in wood. He made for my mother her cabinets and bookshelves. He met her in the shop where she worked, creating designs for wallpaper, fabrics, and tiles. He wanted to sell her a carving he had made, to go with the sign above the door. It was of a swan. She fell in love with the carving, then she fell in love with him. Anyway . . . that's how the story goes.

Oh Diary, why am I telling you all this? Someone needs to know. . . .

A pot of pintos simmers on the cookstove. I call to Raúl, "Get me a cow! I need butter and cheese. I need tortillas!!"

In answer he uses many unpleasant words of language. I hate to see him sleeping on the days he is free from that guardia he joined. When he's not drunk, he strains his eyes over some dumb pamphlet titled "Demolition Devices" or other such idiocy.

He curses and lies like all his borracho friends who brag about the gifts they will buy for me but never do. One will say, grabbing at me as I try to pass to my room, "María, qué bonita!" and they laugh standing in a group with their beards shaking.

"María, there is a song about you."

"María, come here and let me show you how it goes."

They smell of whiskey and their eyes burn with the devil. They are uncouth with small hearts and even smaller minds.

I did the dreaming again last night about my life during the Mediterranean campaign. I wore a braid of gold at my waist, pierced my tongue with a root, and colored my hands red yellow and blue. . . .

Dream Diary One

Esta es mi mente, understanding. We yoke enyugamos the Nao ship at La Reina's edge. This is a new kingdom, not one of my father's and grandfather's yearning. I come to learn the great, gran matemáticas. To join understanding to a vehement desire. My deeds will be recorded on lienzo cloth. Standing on deck, I observe that my crew is restless—they want to disembark and go dreaming independently.

I speak to them in the mixed language of our ancestors and of those to come: Tzotzil, words pouring out from the throat of the land.

"Now we will travel to the Nava high valley, south of this kingdom. The matemáticas is protected there. Carefully/con cuidado. We must remain together in order to endure."

They want to hear more but I can't give more now.

A good crew—reverent, loyal, but wary of me. Wary of my orders and my lenguaje. Still they follow.

Ojo al ojo, eye to the keyhole, I alone go into the Nava to discern duración perpetua, to observe the stubborn resistance of the malinalli grass, wind not knowing which way to blow. . . .

June 1993

Today is my quinceanera. Fifteen turns around the sun. I feel <u>much</u> older . . . like I am fifty-one, instead.

Were my mother alive, were my Grandma here, or even one of my aunts or my sisters, they would organize an extravagant cumpleaños celebration.

The corona of flowers would be placed on my head, specially created of paper petals, folded then dipped into softened beeswax, to form sweetly scented blossoms.

I would invite friends from school (not so many I guess) and a few of the teachers (<u>not</u> of course Mrs. Ball, la directora). Yes! I would invite Sr. Sarasco, Sra. Alarcón . . . maybe even some of my brother's friends, the younger ones. And of course, mi único hermano, Raúl himself. . . . Well, it <u>is</u> a celebration afterall, marking my entrance into womanhood.

Gaah! My poor heart breaks. Why am I so bereft of loved ones? My parents, my Grandma, my dear sister Ysabel.

Julio! Where is Julio?

God in Heaven, I ask you to attend to whom I am left with here!

I should not complain so much Dearest Diary, lest you get bored and refuse to court my confessions. . . .

Yesterday, Sr. Sarasco said that I was growing to be a lovely young woman. I didn't believe him, of course, but was glad he'd said it, for when people say things about me that I don't believe, I know their words can still affect me like spell. . . .

A strange package arrived a few days ago, wrapped in stiff brown paper, addressed to me in mysterious handwriting. Postmarked from Ciudad Juárez.

I know, I think, it must be from my love, my joy, my Julio. But why the unfamiliar writing and no return address? And no letter, no card, no note!!!

Inside I find a cardboard box stuffed full of torn shreds of newspaper, and inside that, wrapped in crinkly yellow cloth, a wooden doll.

What does he think I am . . . a child? He's not much older, only seventeen. His face is soft and no hairs sprout upon his chest.

However, this is no ordinary doll. Carved from wood about a foot in height, she wears a bright blue dress . . . and from under the hem, trimmed in gold, the tips of her red shoes show.

A friend at school told me that dolls with bare feet are good spirits but that dolls wearing shoes are evil.

I don't believe it. This is a good spirit.

Her fingernails are blue. Her thick orange-gold hair is the color of sunset in winter. Her eyes are open but she looks down at the ground. From Heaven, she has been rushed to earth through blazing glory for a special mission? . . . to inspire me!

Her wings are flame-like things of bright yellow rising above her head.

Not a word from Julio, many months now. I am in agony. I thought by now I would have something more secure to report to you, Dear Diary.

I will sleep with this angel in my bed tonight.

Dream Diary Two
The sky is magenta, and the hills to my right burn with yellow fog. I walk alone, shrouded, far from our caravan and the camp of the Moors who lead us out across this desierto demoniaco. All around me, sand, and the bajo hills through which we must pass. Beneath my shroud, mis muslos thighs pulse with the strain. My feet are cracked.

Back in camp I hear mumurando whisperings, that our water supply is diminishing faster than it should. Is there a leak, or a thief, as some surmise?

Soon the light passes and we set off again nado-a-nado, afloat with the stars. We cannot abide untamed rebelliousness of any kind. But I am the guia zurda, the left-handed one. I cannot choose the simple solution—castigo a ejemplo, to set an example.

I must think of a way to make the deviated one

confess, and set her own chastisement.
I need to know why or who has betrayed me?

Spring 1994

Thoughts of Julio distress me. Why no word? It has been too long.

Has he found another love? . . . or gone to that other earth, hovering above or below this one, resplendent with gardens, flowering terraces, liquid fountains, and streams of light ever clear. He talked of a place he had visited in euphorias brought on by peyote. He told me the place is motivated by different laws and that it moves to a different pattern of time. Duración perpetua.

Spirits and genii exist there alongside lesser celestials. The hummingbird, my namesake, feeds in our world on flowers, then passes through the lattice like a spark, slipping through a slit into that other world where it sleeps in the lap of a blind singing angel. . . .

I told him about my dreaming. He <u>seemed</u> to believe me.

Whatever Julio tells me, I believe. He calls me by my secret name. He knows other things about me too, like how I please myself. He says: "Colibri, sweet thing, come here, sit on my lap." And his hands and his gentle words make the crema flow inside me.

We were born in the same month though two

years separated. He moves like serpentine stone feels to the touch. The muscles of his arms are smooth and firm like a snake. I got my menses last year and formed these mounds to delight the eyes of men. Many have tried to engage my heart. Julio was first.

That space is the place where my tears fell onto the page. Mira, Dear Diary, I have drawn circles around them.

Julio must return always to the American Southwest. The last time, he wrote me a love letter every day for a month. You can bet he didn't learn to write such words in his border school or working summers for his brother on oil rigs.

A yellow moon hangs low in the dust of evening. The cicadas grind out incessant questionings. He was never difficult with me. He laughed for no reason. Memories of the scent from the hollows under his arms.

You river of vehement green,
Dream of all enterprise . . .

Raúl cannot tolerate Julio. Julio dropped school this last December to visit here. Julio bends to kiss my knees. Julio's lips are moist and sweet-tasting. He told me he uses Chapstick everyday for two weeks before coming to see me. His tongue is round and smooth when it flows into my mouth like honey. Once he slipped his "Big Red" chewing gum into my mouth and I could feel where his teeth had made dents in it. I swallowed his gum. I told him I wanted a piece of him inside me.

He knew what I meant, but he is careful and respectful and does not press for more.

If he hadn't forgotten his papers, he wouldn't have had to take the old route back through that stinking river at Piedras Negras. God forgive, maybe they shot him just because, from a distance, he looked like someone else.

You hear about things like that. . . .

There is a cross on his chest he calls "a mark of distinction." He said his brother drew it with a knife. Julio wouldn't tell me what he had done to deserve that punishment. I hope it was not a quarrel over some girl.

You ineffable spring of life,
River of vehement green.

He spoke poetry from memory the day we met outside the Biblioteca in Oaxaca. I was waiting for Raúl, but instead I met Julio! . . . who told me soon after, that I was his first love, and that I would be his last.

There is nothing to do now but re-read his letters, and that makes me so sad I want to die. Oh please, God in Heaven, if you are real, make him write to me again.

We used to have a telephone but Raúl wouldn't pay the bills so they turned it off. It is a home for spiders now, on the portal.

After my parents were killed, for several years, I had no power over my grief. I couldn't talk, I couldn't write for months at a time. Grandma did everything to cure me. But it was Julio, finally, who brought me out of my childish ways. He delivered my body back into a world of joy.

I know that death cannot be undone. It happens to everyone. It will happen to me, to Julio, and to everyone I love or feel affection for.

Lo Siento.

Julio makes a delicious fragrance occur in my room whenever I touch myself using the memory of his hands. I touch my breasts the way he touches them, hardly moving his fingers, gently, as if my breasts were rabbits or doves he's trying to tame. There is one long pale hair between my breasts and he told me not to pluck or cut it.

"It is your wisdom," he said.

He writes: "There is not one square inch of you I do not cherish, mi alma. Your mind is fertile and free. The taste of you remains sweet on my tongue and I shun earthly food. My hunger for you is never satisfied. I want to breathe you in and out, boca-a-boca. Every part of your body is sacred. My soul wants to devour your sweetness. . . ."

Two months later, these words:

"I have so much to tell you, to do for you, but my brother will not let me go just now. But soon! He has found someone else he trusts. He shouldn't trust me, because my mind and body belong to you, Colibri. Siempre. You are a mountain of enterprise that appears alongside me wherever I go. Something in you speaks to me. I feel my destiny swirl around me when you are near. You are in every song I hear on the radio. You are in the engine of my truck when I shift gears to mount a hill. You are there when the blades sweep the rain off my windshield."

October 1994

Raúl doesn't know that the morning and the evening star are one.

"What is this Venus you talk about?" he laughs, snatching at gnats.

I point to the big blue-white light near the moon.

He doesn't believe me when I tell him it is really a planet, not a star, the second planet from the sun, and that its place in the sky is "the crossing of two streams," named as such in the map of a universal system developed by our ancestors.

It is my father's mother I speak of as Grandma. She was of Mayan descent, though they had their own name for themselves (not to be written down). They spoke a dialect called *tzotzil,* which she said comes "from the throat of the land." She came down from the Sierra Suchiapa to marry a merchant. They met in June at noon in El Zócalo.

Grandma once told me of the four archangels who hold the reins of the horses that power the universe. Yesterday, in chemistry lesson, I understood what she meant.

My teacher, Señor Sarasco, said that everything in the world—this earth's atmosphere and all the creatures in it and on it, all of the matter or material, including what makes up ourselves— is composed of four basic elements: hydrogen, oxygen, nitrogen, and carbon.

It is just like Grandma said—the four archangels!

Grandma had a potencia with plants. She lived most of her grown life near Las Ollas—about ten kilometers, eagle-wise, from the community of San Cristóbal de las Casas, where she attended church, which is the place where my dear parents died.

Dream Diary Three
Extrañeza! Wonderment. Utmost end!

We have reached what seems to be the edge of earth. Cañon Extremidades. Wider and deeper than any I have seen or imagined.

What is this place? I have not been told of a thing so great. To revive my crew I try to explain this extreme wonderment we feel gazing into the edge of such an immense, clouded, falling away.

Mito, mi guarda, expresses fear in her eyes. What is she thinking? Ambush, snare by demons, ghost souls, foreign types, or jinns of bad mentation. . . .

A man appears, riding a donkey. We have seen men. We have known men before. This man carries a torch of blue-black flame. His hair falls down his back in a thick trenza braid.

I see warm animals crouching inside his eyes.

Walking toward me he opens his hand. Our palms embrace. Dios mío! Nos acaramelamos inmediatamente. Covered in caramel, I am infatuated utterly. I struggle to keep my arms, like snakes, from encircling his face.

Arousal and fear. Intruso intriga.

He directs us to descend into the humo vapour.

"Is water there?" I ask.

"Si, agua puro, but you must not drink."

"Why?" My suspicion increases. "Who are you?"

"Nunca Más."

"Who sent you?"

"Your future," he replies.

I don't abide this manner of speaking. My crew has moved to surround me in a protective arc. They lean forward expectantly. They will accept no more vagaries from the man.

I feel the urge to devour some living thing. What makes me feel at this same instant such unutterable weakness?

My crew sees my vacillation and begins to lose faith.

Something inside this man, or inside me, wants to break free from the path, utterly.

Cara cara, beware, cuidado.

"Adelante!" I say loud enough for all to hear. "Where do we go, hombre? Be clear."

Sensing my inner victory, he capitulates, "I will show you."

My crew accepts this answer. Their approval rises like a wind at my back.

He hands me a sewn-tight ubre. "Drop one into clear water when you wish to eliminate toxicity. It is fine water but you are not conditioned to its metals and radiant elements. If you find a muddy pool you may drink freely without harm. If we become separated, follow the path. I will meet you at the bottom, and you lead on."

I nod in agreement. Blue tentacles cavort inside my belly. As he turns to go, I remove my puñal dagger and slit the udder. Hand inside, fingers know in dark what was puzzling before. It is a simple sarta—a string of pearls, surely of some value. I check the authenticity by running the pearls against the edges of my teeth, noticing the finely-segmented vibration, like waves against a beach. . . .

My eyes follow his braid bouncing upon his back, as he disappears into the fog, riding his burro.

My innards churn. Bancarrota!

Will he lead us to failure . . . or a new start?

December 1995

Went eeling today with my new friend, David. We met ten days ago outside the Museo del Palacio in Oaxaca. Sr. Sarasco had invited a group of students to join him for café . . . I have no idea why I instead preferred to wait on a street corner, looking up at the trees . . . qué misterioso.

A tall, long-limbed, man passed by. I surprised myself by asking him for the time, and we ended up walking and talking. We made arrangements to meet in a week for coffee, which we did. It was nice. He has a long, straight nose, a kind of pale, dusty-colored, wavy hair . . . I like the look of his hair, though it seems a bit untamed. He told me that he is here on assignment from his university back in the United States.

This morning, he arrived in his rented automobile, bringing the poles and bait, and two pairs of green rubber boots. As we drank sweetened coffee from his thermos, and ate little sandwiches made of dark bread spread with slices of salty meat, David (I am christening him "Damasco") said he was proud of me for getting up so early.

Proud of me?

What does he mean. . . .

That was after we had spent hours on the rocks poking our bamboo rods into crevices exposed by the low tide.

Last night, there was a "blue moon." I know

that there are thirteen full moons in a year, only one month has two. Last night was the night. . . .

I asked Damasco, "Why do they call it blue? Why not the thirteenth moon?"

"I think it refers to a certain feeling you get when you stand alone under it at midnight, and your girlfriend lives far away."

H-m-m-m. Was he thinking of a girlfriend back home? He hasn't mentioned anyone special though we haven't known each other long.

He has been very polite with me. . . .

I got a good look at the moon this morning. Like a balloon full of Fanta about to burst over the town of Juchitango.

We drove first to Mitla to view the ruins. I told Damasco about how the church had been built out of the bricks from the ancient temple. We didn't stay long, Damasco was urgent about reaching the turquoise waters at Puerto Angel.

When we arrived, the sky became overcast, and Damasco exclaimed, "This is great fishing weather!"

We walked down a trail to a promontorio. I asked about the green stuff at our feet, covering the jagged volcanic rock.

"Algae. Most seaweed is a type of algae, which eels like to eat. Did you know that diatoms, also an algae, are among the most important creatures in the sea."

"Why is that?" I asked.

"Well, diatoms are important because they are so abundant, they support most of the flora and fauna of the seas. Their shells make up vast tracts of ocean floor. They have unusual forms of reproduction . . . and each single-cell organism is unique, like a snowflake. . . ."

He tugged at his line, continuing, "To me, the most interesting part is . . . each successive generation tends to get smaller, but then . . . sexual reproduction restores . . . significant ecologically because. . . ."

I was getting a bit overheated from his speech, though he has a calm, quiet tone to his voice. I leaned closer, and found myself trying to determine how many shades of green and gold were to be found in his eyes.

I told him how my father built our house.

"The walls are a paste of gypsum and flour, the floors made of sand-cement mixed with bull's blood."

"Bull's blood?" His pole dipped dramatically and he pulled back on it with a snap of the wrist.

He made our poles of bamboo cane stalk with a length of wire fixed to one end, attaching the big hooks he'd purchased from the hardware store.

We bait the hook with a strip of calamari. Damasco shows me how the strip is twisted several times onto the hook so that it will remain in place. The tentacles, removed ahead of time, are tossed far into the water, to distract the crabs.

"It is illegal to keep any crabs you might accidentally catch. This," he insists, "is a santuario."

His Spanish isn't too good, so we mostly converse in English.

"Crabs are smart," he explains. "They never swallow the hook. They just nibble away at the bait until they've got it all."

Struggling and cursing (under his breath) Damasco pulls a large wriggling purplish fish out of the water and drops it, plop!, onto the bank.

Hooray! But . . .

Oh no . . . he can't seem to get the hook out of his eel. Not as smart as those crabs, I guess! He keeps pulling and pulling until something starts to come up. Oh I am so grateful to see that it is in fact the bait and not the poor thing's insides.

Not as ugly as I imagined, the eel gleams an iridescent green with large, pearl-like eyes.

I pat the head of the wriggling animal, saying, "Thank you for your donation to our stewpot."

Damasco laughs freely. He has even, white teeth. He doesn't laugh at me. He reminds me of Julio in that regard. Julio laughed a lot and made me laugh but he never made fun of me. I am fed up with the abuse I get from those bums my brother drags home. "María, bring the beer. María sit down here." I pretend not to hear them. I sneak out and hide in the arroyo until the clouds fill with visions.

Now, something jerks at my line. More pronounced than the gentle nibbling of the crab I had twice felt before.

"Hold it right there. Feel it a few more times. He's got to want it. He's really got to want it. When your line grows heavy, pull back on it hard!" Damasco says, trying to hide his excitement.

I did just as he asked, and out came a long black eel with a golden spot on its neck. Bigger than Damasco's eel!

"Fantastic! Hold it up high over the rocks so it won't wiggle back into the sea."

My eel is hooked cleanly through the lip. I see by the light in her eyes that she has no regrets.

Damasco says he will show me how to clean and skin them when we return to his workshop. I want to learn how to do everything myself. I cannot depend on anyone else.

"Damasco!" I cry out, "They are suffering! We must kill them now."

"How?" he asks, eyes widening.

"You're asking me!? How do you usually do it?"

Hasn't he done this many times before?

I suggest, "We'll hit them on the head with a rock," pointing to a large white quartz near my foot in the dirt.

"Just a moment. I'll find something."

He returns with a branch of manzanita, size of a baby's arm.

"Hold it tight!" he commands, handing the smaller eel to me.

I can hardly hold it for all the slippery slime covering its skin.

A red kerchief placed over the eyes, D. bangs sharply three times.

When the body relaxes in my hand I know it has passed to that other world. Uncovering its limp form, I see a small dent in the forehead.

Back at Damasco's we drop our beauties onto a board and wash them in cold water. Cutting through the skin all the way around just under the gills, Damasco holds each eel by inserting two fingers into the gills, then putting his thumb into its mouth. He hands me the pliers, directing me to pull off every last bit of the dark slippery skin.

I pull and pull until finally we have only the heads to remove. We cut off their heads with a knife, then gut and rinse them. Such smooth white flesh inside that rubbery covering.

We invent this recipe using what we find in his kitchen:

Place two eels head-to-tail, side-by-side, in a glass dish coated with olive oil. Pour one-half cup of milk over fish. Top with chopped chipotles. Bake twenty minutes.

The eels were delicious! Damascus calls them "heels" because his grandfather—who taught him all this—came from Sicily. Since they don't use the letter "h" in their language, D. explains, they are always putting it in where it doesn't belong.

This place is a preserve used by marine biologists. Damasco knows about it because of the people he studies with back home, in San Diego, California. He is only here for a short while, he explains, but he will come back. . . . I'd like to believe him.

April 1996
Here, with Raúl and his buddies, it is always dinero, night and day. I am sick with their talk. Their voices are thick from drink and argument. I have a plan they must never know, a plan that has to do with this land, which I claim as my own. I will study the land, carefully, thoroughly. I will know it inch by inch. I, alone, will know all the plants and animals who live on it, who fly over and nest, who burrow, slither, and glide inside it. In this manner, I will make use of the land without violating it.

Good news! I received another post card from Damasco today. He expects to be returning in June.

June 1996
Dear Diario:
Do you know that Mama left many interesting mementos? I am wearing her locket today. Inside is a tiny photo of my father and one of the baby who died. That boy was conceived in between

Raúl and myself. I might have had another, better, brother had that one survived. Mama couldn't mention him without tears coming into her eyes.

She had no idea, I am certain, that I would peer so intently into the details of her life. I have been re-reading the scrapbooks, showcasing her designs and the prizes she won. Then, there are the letters she saved. I know that she was a passionate woman. She saved the letters from all her lovers. There were quite a few.

Father built this house. An arch forms the main fireplace, five feet across and seven feet deep. Big enough to burn a tree trunk, "or a body," he used to say, joking.

Each room has two windows, on opposite sides. One faces the courtyard where pine boxes hold trees, pear and almond. One faces out to the land. Large copper kettles hang over the black brick stove, which has an "iron companion" my mother often used.

Yesterday, I cooked my first dinner for Damasco. He has been very kind to me. He was appreciative of my lamb stew with tomatillos and the stubby carrots from the garden I planted last year. I baked a corn bread without butter. Oil and lard are easier to obtain. Mama didn't use lard except as a poultice for skin eruptions. Olive oil on the inside, she recommended, for beautiful skin and a lubricated mind.

Chocolate and passion fruit for dessert . . . Mama loved those large egg-shaped fruits hanging on vines from the tops of trees.

I know, too, that she loved my father. Though there is nothing on paper to prove it.

June 23, 1996

Indígenas stop by sometimes looking for Mama. My brother and his friends call them "los vencidos"–the conquered–which seems strange because to me mi hermano, Raúl, and his friends are the defeated ones.

Indígenas are not defeated. They wait for their time to come round again. They know how to wait.

Yesterday, Damasco and I walked out to the farthest edge of the land (near as I can tell from maps and stone markers). I savor the time with him. I am sorry that he will again be returning to the United States.

He asked me to think about coming back with him. "Just for a visit," he persisted, taking my hands in his.

Damasco misinterpreted my silence and asked (incorrectly) in Spanish:

"Are you stuck in the thermos of insecurity?"

That made me laugh, in spite of myself. I am thinking again about my land, about my plan. My mind had been stitched to a familiar problem. How to get money to buy a truck? What type of truck to buy? And, most important, what color? I picture myself driving around all sorts of vehicles, a tractor, a motorcycle. Then I picture myself at the wheel of a truck. . . . I see that it must be a green truck.

D. and I climbed a steep slope, clay rubble crumbling beneath our feet. At top, the arid slopes of the great divide dropped away around us. We were soon on the east side with a view of Villa Flores, famous for its mustard and vanilla. I sat in the shade of a massive dak. Damasco situated himself three or so meters away, fully in the sun, wearing a silly-looking canvas hat. Occasionally, a vehicle passed slowly on the senda below.

The book I carried with me always takes me to a favorite place. This is one from my mother's library, a learned work about ancient Persian mystics. Science or poetry? I do not know. In English, the title goes something like, *Spiritual Body and Celestial Earth,* but it was written in French by a man named Henry Corbin. My mother met him once and he signed the book to her.

Fortunately, since this is esoteric material, Mother left notes in Spanish on the horizons. The idea that excites me most is that the earth is a living entity, with cuerpo, body, and alma, a soul.

I have heard that the ocean is one vast entity, and the land another. Then there is the atmosphere, which responds immediately to the actions of both. Back and forth the three argue and converse.

The narrow waxy leaves of the dak tremble in the wind, releasing their scent. I move close to Damasco, so near that our shoulders touch.

"Am I bothering you?" I see that he is writing in his notebook.

He smiles and places his hand on my head. Then he lets it gently slip down my back to the ends of my hair, making me shiver, estremecimiento!

I read aloud a few words from my book. He explains why he wants to study Sanskrit. He calls it the "mother tongue." I say that ancient Maya is the oldest language. Grandma told me that. She said all the languages derive from it, from back in the days when the continents were one.

Damasco rolls his eyes. They are called "hazel," which is also the English word for a kind of nut I like very much, avellana. I dream of kissing his eyes and sometimes I imagine letting my fingers entwine his soft, sandy hair. He is beautiful, I think, though no one else might notice. Tall and strong in the shoulders, but delicate in the face, like a girl.

His real name is David Ambrose Gentry. He's says he's a scientist. I'm not sure what he studies, he seems to be interested in everything.

Now he is describing snakes he's observed: "Harmless ones usually have stripes all down their length, with a small round head no wider than the width of the body. The king snake has horizontal rings, black and white or yellow and white. The mountain skink has a bright blue tail. It's not a true snake but a legless lizard."

I feel a kinship with the mysterious disappearing creatures that vanish into the rocks: lizards, snakes, toads, and such.

Plants are my closest companions. I know D. knows that I know more about plantas than he does, even if I haven't been to college.

D. likes to talk about what he knows. He doesn't ask many questions.

Grandma taught me plenty. She wasn't loca, as others have said. Maybe they were jealous of her. She was a curandera. I spent most of my days with her in summertime. And afterward, when Mama and Papa were gone, we walked often into the foothills looking for medicines. She knew the Latin names. Her memory for names was legendary. The names on almost any page of the botanical dictionary she could recite and then describe. She made me memorize. I got through the M's before she died. Whenever I made a mistake, she rapped me on the knuckles with her smoking pipe.

No me olvido. Why am I so bereft of family? What kind of plan is this, oh Great Creator God?

I like my new amigo. Damasco has gained access to my heart. More than a friend, almost a brother, the good kind of brother. I think I can trust him. But I need to know more.

Dream Diary Four

We lay on a carpet of serena evening dew.

My mind turns to ice at the thought of what I am about to do. To crush me to himself is what he seeks. I feel it in his flesh.

This was not the plan. I am not to follow a man. Why am I here?

Departure vida? To go tomorrow?

"Dear adorado mío," I whisper in my heart. Only sometimes am I ruthless enough to say those words out loud . . . sincerity, composure, your ardor with me. . . .

"Ovulado! Don't make me cry in front of them."

"We will use the ascensor," he whispers. His tongue lightly touches my ear.

"The what?" I am startled by such closeness.

"There is an elevator here," he strikes his chest with his fist. "You must know it. No?"

I've been waiting my entire life for a surprise from a man.

"This elevator is propelled like a windmill. No mentiro. You must concentrate, use the breath as pulley. One side goes up toward heaven, the other goes down into the earth. The motion of watching makes the wings of the windmill turn."

He squeezes me along his length.

"I tell no untruth. To attain a distance from trouble, from sorrow, disappointment, disillusionment, pain, the elevator operates in a vertical dimension, which means that minutes, hours, days in the elevator may be counted

only a fraction of a second here, on the ground. Skill in using the elevator proves useful."

"And to go down?"

"The ascensor was developed for the purpose of climbing. However, there are many reasons to descend. You will discover them for yourself. One might answer a question or recover something lost. You cannot go down to benefit yourself, or to hide from something you are required to face. You would have no protection from the dangers were you to go down on your own behalf. The universe is biased toward anyone who vows to benefit another. It bends in a protective influence. . . . Going up, however, is entirely for pleasure, for restoration. Pleasure is of benefit to all mankind, to all existence, to every discrete, rare, and unique, without equal, living thing."

I try to pour the sauce of his words onto the agent of my imaginacíon.

"No worry." He says, seeing doubts swarming like gnats about my head. "Mira, I show you."

We climb to a high place in the stratified rocks. One rock is shaped like a banco with a tall back escaño, almost like a throne. We lay side by side on the rim. . . .

. . . He is on the rock with me. Then it seems he is the rock, or the rock is he. I am holding onto a rock, a man, a living thing.

We press our hearts so that our arms contain what, together, we generate. We cling to each other with our legs and arms and feet, a nourishing intermingling—such as the mingling of quinoa with rice—every space in one filled by the other.

In an instant we are combined, blended like milk and water.

I feel things moving about, rearranging themselves inside an atmósfera of serenity.

The elevator is in motion. Soon, there is the swoon, desmayo.

I tell no untruth.

It was how the game of chess, step by step, gains in complexity . . . simple and elegant . . . como the crocheting of a net, spaces and curves of twine interlacing. . . .

We did not descend. However, he introduced me to the technique, in case I might choose to go down later, when needed. He explained:

"You must ask for direction from a spirit guide. The guide might be a plant, an animal, or a person. You will know whom to ask by the fact that she presents herself to you four times. Four times. It might be in dream, in vision, or in realidad."

I ask about my mission.

"I don't know," he says, "I am only a messenger."

June 25, 1996

Raúl and his buddies are stealing again. They load and unload wooden cases filled with many guns. They empty bottles of mescal. They lace-up their boots and pull their caps down low over their eyes. Then they walk out into the night. Rev-up their noisy motors and disappear.

I have asked Raúl many times what the letters stand for: "GS." He tells me not to bother about any of this. He says they are helping the army protect us from foreign invaders.

What a tale . . . Grandma knew how lonely I would be. Before she passed away she taught me to use the mirror of obsidian. It only seems to work when I'm desperate, as I was last night.

The pack of them stood hunched over stacks of U.S. dollars like rats at cheese, quarrelling. They didn't know I was watching. I kept quiet and listened from the pórtico. I heard mention of a "cartel." The cartel must be something like the Marcab Confederation that Grandma warned me about. I knew this was serious.

"Colibri, what is sin?" David often asks. (It's a game we play.)

"Sin is when you take more than you need."

"But what if you get more than you deserve," says he.

Sad for me, he leaves again in a few days.

My brother and his compadres are too stupid to realize they'll be blasted out of existence by those other molestos thieves. Everyone knows they control one whole corner of the universe.

Outside my room, on the south wall of the house, the desmayo is budding. Its bark turning green and glossy.

The mirror of obsidian advises me to make

a big change.

Raúl is a stranger now. I wonder can we really be familia?

One day I watched him reading while I chopped squash for a soup. This is the bad part—his lips move when he reads! I never noticed it before. He was holding a booklet called "Control of Vegetation" issued by the Army Corp of Engineers. That's where he gets all his reading matter.... I guess he is plotting his marijuana crop. He will likely burn down the place trying to clear the land.

Of course, these books are in English, and his English is not so good as mine, but still! He seems muy estúpido now. Once, I'm sure, he was smarter than I.

Descabellado. He is lost.

He licks his thumb each time he turns a page. What happened to his brain? This is the hermano who taught me to play puck-and-ring. Who named the continents and seas for me. Who could spell from memory all the states of our nation. Who carried me on his back and put me to bed at night. Who helped me practice the multiplication tables and showed me how to do long division.

Raúl polishes his boots every day and places them at the foot of his bed. He adores those boots. When he goes to the seashore (hardly ever anymore) he will not step in the sand with his boots on. He walks miles in town to wait all day for some bad man in a café, careful never to step in mud, careful to wipe the slightest bit of dust from his boots using his pocket pañuelo.

This, a man who never washes his hair.

Yesterday, I took a different path, got lost, followed some horse tracks for what seemed like hours, came upon a large slab of black rock, jutting from the greenery, nearly covered over by vines and wild vanilla.

On inspection, I saw a carved stone face, long thick nose, half-closed eyes, una bruja, maybe, or a warrior priest?

Why have I never stumbled across this monstrosity before?

Instead of fear, I felt weak and ashamed like I was secretly growing a baby. I won't tell anyone but you, Diario Mío, about how I sat with my back against the face among the leaves and maguey spines. I felt the warmth flow up from mi flora privada to the top of my head.

A flickering strip of sunlight, the sound of insects, like little electric saws with their clicks and whirring motions, created such a strong instant flow of enjoyment I soon had my pleasure, which gained and gained in strength. I was afraid it would not stop.

When I gave out a sharp gasp, a lizard near my foot burst alive and disappeared beneath a bruised agave. . . . I remembered the colossal head of La Venta in Tabasco, carved by the oldest inhabitants of the land. Twenty-five tons it weighs. David took me to see it.

It didn't affect me the way this one did today. Cabeza a cabeza. . . .

David said it was a surprise that <u>any</u> of the treasures of pre-Columbian peoples are still around, available for public view.

"It means there are a few honest men."

I was blissfully alone all day yesterday. Unfortunately, on the way back home I began to worry about Raúl. . . .

This erased my former exceptional enjoyment.

At twilight, feeling my solitude, soledad, I dragged Raúl outside to view a last display of rainbow light among the clouds on the horizon.

"Ah," he said, smiling a little, in the dark, as clouds covered the rising moon. The air became suddenly breathlessly still, as the birds ended their evening song.

I reminded myself that Raúl was indeed mi hermano and how once upon a time I had fiercely adored him. He took me everywhere with him before the hairs grew on his chin. He confided in me, taught me songs to sing.

I saw in his slow smile, as his eyes flickered with the departing light, that deep inside we were still those same ones. . . .

I walked alone down the sandy arroyo heading south from the house.

. . . Tonight the moon makes the path glisten.

Grandma blamed much on distilled liquors. In her land, the caciques at first controlled the sale of mountain-brewed alcohol when it was made in the fermented tradition and used for ceremonial purposes. But later, when it was distilled, it became too potent for most people.

She said there was nothing wrong with drink in itself—it enhances pleasure and allows a necessary forgetfulness that may be a requirement for living a long and productive life. A strong-minded person will not succumb to alcoholism, she said, because a strong-minded person perceives, fairly quickly, that the pleasure must be regulated or it turns to torment.

"But now," she told me, "most people have so much pain and fear inside, they have no strength to resist the alleviating properties of distillate." And so they cannot stop once they begin. A powerful "spirit" takes over.

Her people had an injunction against the fifth cup. Only priests and ceremonial leaders were allowed a fifth cup. Drunkenness was strictly forbidden . . . that is, until degenerate caciques gained power over men's souls in an attempt to weaken the will of the populace, in order to amass personal wealth for themselves.

Distillate helped them accomplish their goals.

She told me that the Church attempted to break this hegemony, claiming that rampant alcoholism contributes to violence. However, Chamulans who converted to Catholicism, or joined the rising force of Protestantism, were equally in danger for their lives.

Mi madre y mi padre were killed visiting Grandma, during an attack on the cathedral of San Cristóbal. Nineteen people died that day.

Grandma died a few years later, of poisoning. She had been a vocal opponent of riotous fiestas, and the corrupt bosses who encouraged or allowed the killings. Her own curé powers were useless against a powerful medicine injected into her tobacco, which immediately stopped her heart.

Grandma told me to keep a watch on Raúl. She had observed his lack of direction and his excessive use of intoxicants.

"He will end his life with a knife in his back or a bullet in his brain."

She explained how the Zapotec forgot their true beginnings by embracing the new Mixtec traditions. The great Mayan society, itself, early-on lost track of the source of its wisdom, embracing materialism and a disregard for human life.

"The history has yet to be written," she said, explaining that the remaining elders of Shoshoni and Hopi tribes in Los Estados Unidos are guardians of some of the truths about mankind's history and its end.

"Peligroso, darker than the time we are in," she moaned, tapping the ashes from her pipe.

She taught me to make soap from the copalxocotl. She taught me to boil the porous roots, along with the little yellow flowers, over slow coals for twelve hours to make the salve that relieves pain. The paste is dried in the sun under dampened hemp cloth.

Uses of the maguey are many, aside from the ritual drink: green leaves are crushed and the fibers separated to produce a fabric that can be made into a rough cloth for washing, or a fine cloth, like linen. The spines make good needles. Shoots nearest the earth are delicious when cooked. Dried leaves make a smokeless fuel and the ashes can be used as a poultice.

She made me memorize these things by placing them on my fingers. I know there were six but I only have retrieved five. . . oh yes, the sixth is pulque itself – how forgetful the name makes one.

June 27, 1996 – Cumpleaños

In a few hours I will be eighteen. I can hardly wait to be old. What is the sense in being young when life seems turned upside-down.

Damasco stayed on to celebrate my birthday.

I hate to admit how I doubted him.

He is twenty-two years old but seems sometimes like an old man . . . or a child.

I stayed home today to listen to Mother's old albums. (D. fixed the record-player, last time he visited. He used a rubber band!)

One song made me so sad, I played it over and over. I will play it for Damasco. He is coming to spend the night.

Raúl has been gone for awhile. Who knows where. . . .

I want tonight to be perfect. Damasco wants to cook for me. He will make pollo and greens and he is bringing a taro root beer he says he invented himself. When the moment is right, I will play the song for him, which was written by Cole Porter and recorded in Cleveland, U.S.A., by Steve Lawrence:

> *Do you love me*
> *as I love you . . .*
> *Will you change my life,*
> *or will this dream of mine*
> *fade out of sight . . .*
> *Like the moon growing dim*
> *on the rim of the hill*
> *in the chill*
> *still of the night.*

Damasco and I have not made love. I told him I want to. He says I'm too young. He says he's "not ready." I don't know what that means.

Julio wasn't like that. Julio was always ready. Julio asked all the time, with his persistent gentle manner. Nonetheless, Julio respected my reserve.

I was the one who wasn't ready then. . . .

Now, I am ready.

Damasco keeps asking me to return with him, to visit his family in California. I am afraid.

I said I will not even think of it until he has made love to me. Then I will know.

What if I never see Raúl again in my entire life? Awful as he is, he is my own, and only, familia. He needs me to protect him from the harm he brings on himself.

This past spring I got my diploma. I was able to spend more hours working at la tiendita, trying to save enough money to buy a truck, so that I might easily get there and back without depending on anyone. My job is in Zaachila, just outside Oaxaca. I work at the Ramirez Family Grocery and Feed. I am cashier. When the calculating register breaks down, I am the only one who knows how to properly make change.

I have always been supreme at matemáticas.

After the work day is done, I walk in the gardens among orchids and lilies. Damasco has received a research stipend, which he says means he "gets paid to goof off." He says his latest interest involves the origin of the nomenclature of plant classifications in New World species. New World, Old World, what's the difference? This has always seemed like an old world to me.

D. says I am to be a help to him with names

and plant identifications, knowing by heart many of the common names, as well as the Latin.

D. describes the house he grew up in: "Long ranch-style with a split pine fence surrounded by corrals for the horses."

Corrals for the horses! That sounds nice. But here we like our courtyards, all the life goes on within. . . .

D. says his house is more like a train, rooms in a row like train cars.

Damasco's parents were horse breeders. Then his father died. His mother, Karen, and her cariño, Clive, "play polo and travel the world." D. tells me that they are members of an exclusive club that admits only the wealthy and influential.

D. says I might not like them at first, but at heart they are good people.

They live near San Diego, in Rio Hondo. His uncle owns a house across the bay from San Francisco, in a town called Tiburon. Tiburon means "the shark." So many names D. mentions are in español: Fresno, Yerba Buena, San Francisco, Los Angeles. I think I might like California.

Damasco believes Raúl will eventually be killed or put in jail. There is no doubt about it. This makes me desesperada. How can I abandon him?

Also, my land needs me. I have not finished with my investigations. . . .

D. says he will help me buy a truck, or whatever

I need. He wants me to agree to go back with him to Estados Unidos, very soon! Just for a visit, he keeps repeating. I don't know what to do.

Diario Mío, what do you say? I have no one to advise me but you.

I fear the word you utter is cuidado. . . take care.

I tell D. about the world's oldest living tree, the famous cypress growing in the churchyard of Santa María del Tule. Fifty meters high and at least 4,000 years old.

"I have never seen it and can we visit next week? And what about Monte Alban, the ruins?" These are things I need to do before I make any rash decisions.

Monte Alban overlooks the entire Oaxacan valley. I need to see it from such height.

Damasco hasn't been there either. He doesn't know much about Monte Alban, but he says yes, yes, yes, to whatever I ask.

I walk out across the solid ground of my plot of dirt while the sun crawls soñolentamente toward earth. A dragonfly alights on a spray of jungle geranium, allowing me to view the delicate design on the wings. Sage and wild ginger scent the breeze. The moon hesitates at the crest of the hill and I stand transfixed by a sudden display of harmony . . . interpreting it as message for what I am to do.

Nuevo Día, Nuevo Mundo, June 28, 1996
Lux aeterna. Líbrame. Yesterday, I heard for the first time the Verdi Requiem.

Last night we made love.

Damasco gave me a bottle of scent, Chypre, from Paris.

I asked him not to pronounce the word. It is so beautiful as printed on the label.

I wrote this for him:

Last night you said I was a desert in spring. You said I was a forked road, a forked branch, a vase-turned upside down to hold the sun. You said I was polished sticks of different lengths and thicknesses, the sagebrush tumbling across the chaparral. You said all this, but not with words. I want you to know it is what I felt too, though I said nothing. And you were the rain running down the seams in a rock, the rain pouring into a dry creek bed, gathering into a stream, rushing to become a river with living creatures inside, spilling over me, all over me and through me, on your way back out to sea.

1997-1998 Notebooks: David Ambrose Gentry

Tiburon, CA:

Soon returning home to rescue academic work after weeks of blissful ocean, fog horns, and Colibri. Uncle Bob let us stay. He's in Turkey.

Colibri says she would like to live here someday.

For me it's too white, too clean, too orderly.

Two kinds of chaos: the one we fear and the one we crave.

Tiburon, "the shark," she says. The entire promontory was once owned by a single Spanish family. Now it's subdivided. Modest house on quarter acre sells for two and a half mil. Sundays, bankers and CEOs cruise in Jaguars and Porsches. Weekday mornings they line up in suits to board the express ferry to San Francisco. Clutching their neatly folded *Wall Street Journals.*

Yesterday C. and I walked down the hill (past the cleverly disguised sewage treatment plant at the corner of Mar East and Paradise). Even the buff-grey rip-rap at dock's edge is sparkling. As if it was recently extruded from some high-class rip-rap factory. Groomed women in spandex and sun-hats sip coffee, overlooking the green-grey Bay.

Off in the distance, white-washed towers and

spires. "Prettiest city in the world." Soon to be our new home.

I was surprised to see a bum outside the café asking for change.

A fallen god, abandoning his people, covered himself in ashes and moved among them as if he were lost—half-remembered poem fragment came to mind.

I watched the bum get the surprise of his life. One "suit" peeled off a twenty, handed it to him.

"How did I talk myself into this?!" bum says out loud. Not a bad-looking guy. New-ish sneakers. What would you expect from upscale Tiburon?

Inside, bum pleads, "Can I have one cup here, then a refill to go?"

Owner, diplomatic but firm, "One cup here, then you go."

"With a refill to go?"

"With a refill to go."

He moves to prime table by the window, sits quietly in the sun. Expressing, in his own way, perfect heart and countenance. I feel for him.

— 1.22.97 RELATIONS

Angel Island. No one lives here but park rangers. Entire island dedicated to "a natural habitat." Clear sky all the way to the top. Stunning view of fog roiling in through the Golden Gate. It does "roll in." Just like they say.

Descending, C. and I linger at an overlook. Watch sailboats tip wildly in the rough bay. C. is fascinated by the tiny white flowers among mosses and ferns. Blossoming under dense trees. Winter's the green time here.

Caught the ferry and continued on to San Francisco. Riding the bus up Russian Hill, we met an old woman, from Honduras. She and Colibri conversed rapido in Spanish (C. occasionally pausing to translate for me).

The old lady lives in the St. Francis of Assisi house on Guerrero. She injured her spine a while back. Is now in constant pain. Colibri wants to do something for her. Promised to bring her a remedy. Something her mother used to give the indígenas.

"A salve made from the testes of male jackrabbits," C. says, straight-faced.

We stopped into a photo exhibition. Large black & white photos of Mexican nationals who had illegally crossed into the U.S. All were caught and detained or sent back. Documented by a professional photographer.

I wonder how they feel about having their faces enlarged and hung on these pristine gallery walls. Anglos gawking.

C. stood for a long time in front of one. "Unidentified Man." Dark-skinned broad-shouldered youth with penetrating black eyes, looking straight out of the frame. Long gleaming wet hair. Fresh from the river. I tried not to notice how many times she returned to that photograph. She told me it reminded her of her first love, Julio. (She hasn't seen him in over five years.)

"Maybe he's alive in jail . . . or they sent him back?" she asked me.

The wall text stated that some of the men escaped.

I sensed how much she had loved him. I was jealous of that fact. Jealous, too, of her ability to love. So young. It was true what Mom had said about me. I had never really been in love. At least not that way. Until now.

No scenes. No hysteria. She's like that. Dignified in her suffering.

Have read about how teenage "mules" hired on the streets of Las Palomas carry 50-pound packs of marijuana and cocaine across the border. And the heavy trafficking in illegal immigrants. Hidden in the backs of trucks and vans, along with stolen antiquities and archeological treasures.

Recently, I read a vehicle was apprehended carrying a stash of paintings (from World War II Nazi caches), Tibetan treasures, Mayan jade figures, and a petrified dinosaur egg.

Wondered if this might explain the disappearance of Julio. Must be quite a temptation.

Back in Uncle Bob's glassed-in heaven. Two

fog horns sound, intermittently, in the distance. One: long and low. The other: two short, high bursts. Occasionally they come into phase. The long, low horn chases the high one. Finally catching up. Slowly they separate again. Punctuated by the cries of sea birds.

I'd purchased a vial of ylang-ylang in Chinatown.

"For centuries," the lecherous old herbalist said, speaking directly to C., "it was used as love potion. Takes 400 pounds of flowers to produce one pound of oil."

Colibri said she liked the scent. In her hair, on her shoulders, irresistible.

She had snipped two orchids from the sundeck. She brushed my chest all over with one. Then, I watched as she made use of the other, flicking it against her clitoris. Two pale-tipped fingers holding her delicate lips apart.

The sounds she made were musical and unselfconscious. I've never been with a girl with such a natural sensuality. As we made love, a ferocity in me threatened to overwhelm the mood.

I was afraid my need would change the subtle sensations into something coarse.

— 2.1.97 S.I.N.

"Traditional" recipe from C.:
Sangrecita
- 1 quart lamb's blood
- 1/2 pound diced lamb liver
- 1/2 pound diced lamb heart
- 1/2 pound sliced bone marrow
- 1/8 teaspoon oregano
- 5 cloves garlic crushed
- 1/2 teaspoon red chile seeds
- 1/2 teaspoon salt
- 1 tablespoon lard or oil

Boil the blood for one-half hour. Fry the liver, heart, marrow in the lard. Combine blood, seasonings, and fried mixture. Cook another hour. (Is this some kind of love potion?)
— 2.9.97 S.I.N.

Rio Hondo: Colibri got me looking into yucca. Saponin—a glucoside—is found in the roots. Good for washing. Extracting the fibers, an abrasive powder is obtained. Used in toothpaste and scouring compounds. Chenopodium stems also contain saponin (Chenopodiaceae—goose + foot —name derived from shape of leaf). Extracted glucose is used in candy, alcoholic fermentation, and leather tanning. A softening, loosening agent. Strange how an agent that cleanses, loosens, purifies is also used in the creation of synthetic sex hormones. (The glycerin/ester link:

COO-COO-COO, sound of doves?)

Argument with Professor Ames, visiting from UC Berkeley. He says 99% of the pesticides we consume occur naturally in plants. Nature's attempt to keep pests away. Synthetic chemicals have the same effect as natural ones. All are potentially cancer-causing at high doses.

With you so far, old man.

He goes on to insist that organic vegetables are *potentially more hazardous* than ones grown with conventional agricultural methods. Here's why, says he. The organic strains have developed natural pesticides as a resistance. And those chemicals cannot be washed off, are in fact endemic causing the plant to be—though rich in nutrients—potentially poisonous. Tests with the proverbial "rats" would prove the natural chemicals to be equally carcinogenic. It's just that nobody bothers to extract and test them.

"Hey," I say, "extract of rat would cause tumors in rats if the injections were large enough." I mention the fact that conventional agricultural methods create highly inferior strains. Plant fiber is weakened by excessive use of chemical fertilizers (derived from petroleum), the famous NPK. And new strains are particularly susceptible to invading insects or viruses, which in turn have grown stronger with successive generations, leading to increased need for stronger pesticides.

Furthermore, in the presence of artificial nitrogen, the natural "fixation" of nitrogen—from the air by soil bacteria—ceases. Which makes it increasingly difficult for food producers to give up the use of artificial additives.

Addiction. Depletion. Disease.

"It has been proved," I insist, "that the vitamin and mineral content of food grown by agri-business has diminished significantly over decades."

Ames sighs. Continues arguing his case. "Since agri-business technologies have allowed more fruits and vegetables to reach the consumer at a lower price, more people can afford to eat more of them more often. Therefore, since it follows that because fruits and vegetables (grown with pesticides *or* without) are known cancer inhibitors, the use of pesticides actually contributes to lowering the cancer rate."

Dazzling logic. But he comes off as a pompous old fool anyway.

He spent most of his life eating natural produce and free-range chickens and pigs that were the mainstays of pre-World War II life. *He* grew up in a world free of "better living through chemistry." *He* wasn't spoon-fed high-fructose corn syrup chemical-laced phyto-toxins like *my* generation.

A final in thermodynamics tomorrow. The word itself intimidates me.

Next month we move into our own apartment. San Francisco. Rose Street.

— 2.20.97 NAMING

Picked up Colibri outside the University Biology Dept., where she's been working as "research associate" six weeks now. She's basically a glorified secretary. But she likes the job. Gets asked to do a variety of things. Likes learning to use the computer. Is adept at filing and catching mistakes. Good at diagrams. She's drawing up a chart for a professor now, delineating groupings of the numerous varieties of *Zea mays*.

True "maize" is one of the most highly specialized grasses in the world. There were once wild varieties, but cultivated forms filled those niches. Wild varieties eventually died out. Native Americans, through intentional cross-breeding, produced this marvel. Thousands of years before the arrival of Europeans. Subspecies, *mays,* is borrowed from the Spanish.

Our common name, "corn," is believed to have arrived with English pioneers, due to the dried kernels being similar to "the tough formations on the weary traveler's feet."

C. works hard and I know they like her there. Colleagues have commented on how smoothly the office runs since her arrival.

There's one young post-doc who wants to

jump her bones. I've surprised him several times, leaning on her desk. Making a pest of himself. Always has a hand-rolled cigarette behind his ear. Pretentious grin. Asks too many questions. Wants to know things he doesn't need to know. About her background, her life in Mexico, her family, etc. . . .

She tells me he's just being conversational (*not* her type she assures me).

I don't trust him or his motives.

I'm aware, and it disturbs me, that Colibri might feel lonely. Missing her old friends, her teachers. Even that rat of a brother.

C. secured her own stipend for summer. Assisting in the field with an experiment. Paid for, unfortunately, by a commercial producer. Testing a "magnetic" soil additive. (Sounds like a hoax to me. The additive is nothing more than mica and ferrous ions.) She'll be responsible for incorporating the material, planting the rows of beans, measuring germination, and plotting the rate of growth against untreated controls.

— 1.2.98 NAMING

FROM THE WASHINGTON POST:
Ancient Greeks and Romans had an effective and widely used oral contraceptive: the sap of a plant that once grew in North Africa, which is believed to have been harvested to extinction. The plant

was known as silphion *by the Greeks and* silphium *by the Romans. A variety of giant fennel, it grew in the hills near Cyreme, the ancient Greek city-state. According to records, it was a valuable export crop, worth more than its weight in silver.*

Pliny the Elder mentions silphion's high cost and Hippocrates records failed efforts to cultivate the plant in Syria. The ancient physician, Soranus, wrote explicitly of the plant's uses: He gave several prescriptions for preparing the sap to be taken by mouth, saying it could either be used to prevent conception or cause early abortion. Cyreniac juice, as Soranus called the concoction, may thus have been a "morning after" drug.

The May-June issue of American Scientist, *reports that extracts of surviving relatives of silphion have proven effective contraceptives in experiments with rats* [rats again] *suggesting that some extracts block fertilization while others prevent implantation.*

How could such useful knowledge have disappeared? I asked C. if she knew of any herbal contraceptives. I remembered that when we were first together she had mentioned her "protections." Today she said she didn't *believe in* "contraceptions," which got us into a snag. Until I realized she meant, "contradictions."

I told her that the article states that such knowledge survives in parts of the world where midwives are common: known contraceptives and abortifacients include wormwood, African Commiphora (source of the resin myrrh), the common herb "rue," and nutmeg in large doses. Dried seeds of "Queen Anne's lace" are used in North Carolina to this day.

C. turned away. Didn't seem interested.

Strange dream last night. I'm not in it myself, but Colibri appears, as The Teacher, an older version of herself:

Distant future. Doctor, on board some kind of space ship, questions The Teacher: "Some of the men are asking about their bodily projectiles. We want to know, are they tools or weapons?"

Doctor explains that the crew has lost a million years of evolutionary knowledge in an instant. Language has been retained, but not meaning.

The Teacher says that outside assistance will be required. She consults some kind of authority (a blue fog inside a glass tube), who gives the okay.

The Teacher explains that the crew, individually, must undertake an extreme labor. Each alone must begin to attempt to reconstruct the elaborate tapestry of civilization. Working from the body out, each is to reconstruct his or her own impulses and urges, examine them, weigh them, name them. . . .

— 1.4.98 NAMING

New World foods introduced to the Old World:
chili (from the Nahuatl *chilli)*
chocolate (from the Aztec *xocalatl*)
cocaine (leaves of the *coca* tree, from the Quechua *cuca*)
potatoes (from the Taino *batata*)
cigar (Mayan *sikár*)
tobacco (Taino *tabaco*)
tomatoes (Nahuatl *tomatl*)
vanilla (Spanish *vainilla,* "little sheath," see: Latin *vagina*)
— 1.19.98 NAMING

Tiburon:
Uncle Bob is off again. To Afghanistan this time. Want to know more about what he actually does. Tall, fair-haired, good-looking. Colibri treats him like a god. A bachelor now, he was married briefly years ago. Works for the State Department. That's all he'll let on. He's got a large locking file system, taking up one whole wall in his office. Nothing to be discovered by pouring through his desk drawers (I've tried). Lots of fancy Strathmore stationary with his name letterpress printed in the upper left-hand corner. Expensive electric pencil sharpener. Maps. Many maps.

C. and I are the only ones allowed to stay in his house. He trusts me. He adores her. He said she must be "some kind of angel."

Checking in with a friend at the Romberg Center, who's doing research on complex food webs. Instead of the "six degrees of separation" model, she believes there are only *two* among species populations sharing a habitat.

Sharing a habitat. Me and Colibri. We walk evenings up to the nature preserve. Holding hands. Staring out across the bay. Fog over the foothills.

Colibri asks about my childhood.

"I'm still in it."

"Do all names in California come from the Spanish? You know, like Tiburon."

Hadn't thought about it but, obviously, this was Mexican territory.

She says there's a Tiburon Island on the mainland side of the Sea of Cortez. She visited once. Also there's an Isla Angel de la Guarda on the Baja side. Uninhabited except for lizards and snakes. Similar to Angel Island here. Itself uninhabited by any large mammals except for deer that swam over from the mainland. Early 19th century.

"What is the name of that island?" she asks.

"Alameda."

"See. . . . Spanish again. It means, poplar grove."

I enjoy so much the sound of her voice when she tells what she knows.

C. helps me identify species and their uses. Manzanita, Pacific Madrone, Wild Iris.

"Wild Iris can be used to create a strong poison if you wish to kill someone," she offers, narrowing her eyes.

Iris, Greek goddess of the rainbow, messenger from the gods, the colored portion of our eyes. Iris, my Iris . . . she's certainly wild when she wants to be.

Currant bush. Coast huckleberry. Huckleberry useful for persistent cough, she explains.

She says there is a little aura around each plant that betrays its *familia*. I watch her lips move and forget to write down what she says. She has the sweetest lips I have ever tasted. Her skin is caramel smooth, like those candies Mom used to put in my stocking at Christmas. Firm with a melting sweetness.

We pluck wild raspberries and eat some on the spot. She uses her scarf to carry some back. "We will freeze for Mom and Clive," she says somewhat hesitantly.

They plan to visit soon. They seem perpetually confused about what I chose to do, by marrying C. and living in San Francisco.

Colibri feels it.

I'm changing with her. Where's the dumb dog playing in the river?

Where are my refined cognitive illusions?

Doubts? I am full of them.

— 3.10.98 NAMING

There's a projected future I use as a template. It changes in terms of use of tools. Inhabited by various goals and desires from the past. A melding of intent. Like a novel someone wrote and is continuously rewriting.

Chapter eleven took place today.

I saw a girl. Her hair fell down in front of her eyes. Streaks of dark in the light. I watched her pull her hair down across her face and stumble toward me. She brushed up against me as she passed.

I was buying apricots at a fruit stand.

I felt very strange watching her stumble toward me as if I had read the book before and knew what was coming.

I knew she would brush up against me.

I knew I would not see her face. And that she would disappear around the corner without a word.

I knew that I would feel this way. As if something significant had occurred.

I saw my life as if I had seen my life already. This was a part of my life to come. It was a telepsychotic instant projected onto linear reality. My unformed relationship with that woman moved me into a non-linear reality. An opening in the architecture of time. As if there were slots or louvers at the back of the event. And if you turned those louvers you would see what was going on behind, or alongside, this reality.

Maybe the soul is a time machine.

C. has alluded to this kind of thing. I have not experienced it before.

I'm experiencing shock waves. There is terror involved.

It's like a dream. Of living in San Francisco, perhaps without Colibri. Another time, another form of me. I feel that if I'm not careful I will go into that future or past without taking my current consciousness along.

— 3.20.98 RELATIONS

Colibri was murdered on March 21, 1998

DIARY:
Colibri, California
1996–1998

San Diego Aeropuerto, July 6, 1996

I am María Cuerno y Saeta. Cuerno was my father's name, which means horn or tip as in the crescent moon. I feel that I am now balanced on the tip of that crescent moon. David wants to get married right away, but I don't know. So much has happened already.

The minute we crossed into Texas, I began to miss my land. Also, I was overcome with feelings, remembering my dear sister Ysabel, my ally, so wrongly dead from a car accident. My parents took me to visit her, in her border town, when I was seven-and-a-half. Ten years my senior, she always protected me from Raúl's teasing. She fed me and bathed me when I was a baby. She sang to me and called me her "living doll." Ysabel met her husband young and moved away to be with him, while he was working in the oil fields. It all came back to me when I saw those hammerheads pumping in the red haze. That was a happy time, when they were all alive.

Yesterday we abandoned the bright green Ford truck in Socorro, Nuevo Mexico, in the dirt parking lot at back of the Church of San Miguel. I went inside to pray, though I can no longer truly believe in the bloody God of the Catholic faith.

We had spent the previous night in the bed of our truck under a moonless canopy of stars outside a town called Artesia in the "valley of seven rivers." At Carrizozo we knew Hondo was dying. (I named the truck Hondo for the profound sound of his deep eight-cylinder engine.) We were grateful to be able to coast into the churchyard. David said that someone around there would be happy to have it and fix it up for themselves. We left it, with the keys in the ignition. At a little coffee shop on the plaza, a man, overhearing David's inquiry about busses to Albuquerque, drove us to Soccoro's small aeropuerto, and, just to be nice I guess, provided us with a ride in his airplane. There was barely room for the three of us!

Albuquerque made me think of Mexico City, planted as it is on an elevated plain below ragged peaks. I prefer the small Cesna to that muy gordo United Airlines plane that brought us here to California. The Cesna seemed safe, like riding in a small winged basket. The ground looked as it does when I fly in dreams. . . .

I saw a boy riding his bicycle.

I saw jackrabbits fleeing from the shadow of the plane.

I saw old volcano craters and the wide curving gash of the muddy Rio Grande.

In the jumbo jet, we crossed two states in less

than two hours, to land once again at the edge of my old friend, the Pacific Ocean. Mostly we were above the clouds. I didn't want to look out the window. The clouds made me sad, as though we were at the hem of heaven, where so many of my loved ones have been taken.

Rio Hondo is where we are to live for now. Next to the river, just outside another place named for a saint, San Diego. So many saints in this land. David says we will have our own apartment at his family estate. It is large, he assures me, and we won't be in anyone's way. And it is only temporary, he insists. "Besides," he grasps my hand for emphasis, "Mom and her main squeeze, Clive, are often away."

I guess I am to become David's "main squeeze." For now, we sit on a painted wooden bench in the humid stench of automobiles waiting for the arrival of the Airporter, which will drive us into the city. David phoned his mother to say that we are on our way. . . .

San Diego, July 27, 1996
Tomorrow, we apply for a "green card" for me. Yesterday we stood in the office of a City Hall judge who wore a black robe and a baseball cap. He was an exceedingly large man whose belly rose and fell as he laughed. He seemed quite jolly. I was surprised by how informal it all was.

We listened to his little speeches. We signed all the forms. Then he said that as soon as my papers were verified, we would be officially "hitched."

In Spanish, we call it desposado, which means both handcuffed and newly married. In English they say "wedlock," which also gives a note of uncomfortable binding. . . .

David's family wants to like me, it is clear, but they do not seem to understand why David brought me here.

He is worried, I think. Last night he said he was <u>too tired</u> even to kiss.

"Too tired to kiss?" I asked, feeling a stinging hurt from him, for the first time ever. How can anyone be too tired to kiss?

I know what he was thinking, "What if she gets pregnant?"

His mother had asked at dinner, "What about your degree?"

I don't like using protections. I prefer that we are careful, until the time is right . . . if that time is ever to come. I have explained to David that I know how to prevent making a baby but he does not believe me. Many ancient people knew the uses of las plantas to prevent conception, I said.

"Prove it," was his reply.

That is why I had to divulge some things that my grandmother taught me, and then I found myself telling him about what happened when I was nine years old. I confess it to you, Dear Diary, with a little more detail.

It occurred in the newly reconstructed church at San Cristóbal. I was with Grandma and Grandpa who went there to pray for the recently departed souls of my parents. When they were finished praying, I asked them to leave me alone for awhile. There were some things I wanted to converse with God.

They agreed to return in half an hour.

When the door closed I found myself alone in the darkness. I heard a distinct voice telling me that I must take off my clothes and dance among the pews. If I did it quickly, no one would know. I would be able to guarantee, by this act, that my parents would live eternally in heaven and not burn in hell fire.

I believed the voice. I had heard that voice before.

I don't actually believe in hell anymore, but back then I was afraid to ignore the voice in such a holy place at that particular moment.

I also worried that the priest might suddenly return from his sanctum, or that my grandparents would change their minds and come back for me early.

Was this the voice of the Devil? I had heard it before when I was very small and I don't remember exactly what it said but I know if I did what it told me to do and I was made happy.

My clothing seemed to fall away and I found myself swimming through the air, my arms waving wildly like a windmill in a storm. The soles of my feet slapped against the stones. My feet carried me to the sacristy where I climbed up onto the velvet. Everything was in perfect order and there were a certain number of breaths I needed to count. I think it was nine, my age at the time. Then, I was to lay down flat between the lighted candles under the painted statue of Christ and listen carefully. . . . Something important was about to occur.

I would be returned to a perfectly restored earth where my loving parents would attend me, and my brother would become a doctor, or el presidente, and everyone would live forever. . . .

Feeling this opening of my heart, like a horizon opens before you cresting a hill, a small sharp heat descended into my entrails. I thought for a moment that I might need to defecate upon the dark soft cloth, which seemed like a good idea at the time. . . . I was wandering in my mind through green pastures, where cows with full udders were moving in motion toward me with their sympathetic animal eyes. . . .

The swollen feeling came into my mouth as I have only felt a few times in my life. I heard my own voice saying out loud,

larlept lo-ula leh leh lalo-la . . .

Sunlight pierced the aisle.

My grandfather shouted, "María, Dios!" and rushed toward me.

The immense green pasture rolled up like a window shade, leaving a burning wire that tightened around my lungs so that I couldn't breathe or swallow.

Grandpa treated me badly. I won't linger on what he did right then.

But later, I heard Grandpa telling his version of the story. How he'd found me naked on the velvet, babbling nonsense, my hands roaming my body. We were all standing in the courtyard and my brother and my uncle and several other men were listening to his report on this unfortunate incident.

Their dark laughter cut me worse than razors, worse than a whip.

After that, Grandpa made me stay alone in the cellar for two days. But first he spanked me so thoroughly I could not sit. I knew then that he was wrong in treating me that way.

Grandma did not come to my rescue. Strong though she was, her husband ruled her. At night, I heard them arguing above my head. I knew better than to try to explain to them about the voices and the instructions and the swaying cow udders. . . . Grandma told him I was "una clarividente," a clairvoyant, and she excused my behavior because I was still a child and so recently orphaned. She said that I was probably, for those moments, loca. And she also explained that I, being almost ten, would begin my menses soon (if I was like the other women in our familia) and perhaps that was the reason afterall. . . .

He shouted, "Puta! Puta!" and stomped his feet. I didn't know whether those words were meant for Grandma or me. Or for both of us.

At that moment I remembered what I had recently learned in school, about the sudden appearance of a supernova, thousands of light years away, clearly visible in the night sky near the north star. My teacher had said that some people believe "special human beings" come into existence as a result of that type of luminous cloud.

The thought of that supernova, so distant and powerful, gave me solace.

When I called out in the night, Grandpa came with a crock of water and a dipper. He said he was afraid to leave me alone with a glass.

He didn't say more, but I saw tears behind his eyes, and knew that he was sorry.

Some time later, Grandma told me that when they carried me out of the church into the street my pupils were greatly enlarged and that is how she knew I was enrapto and could not be held responsible for my deeds. She said to the men that I was a confused orphan and should be pitied.

Then, just to be safe, she explained to me

mysteries and techniques, including the methods that my family's women have used for centuries to prevent bringing a child into the world. There are herbs and watching the calendar, and a special trick of the mind that requires some practice and a brief initiation ceremony. She learned it all from her mother.

D. seemed shocked by all this. He didn't say anything but I could tell he was upset. I decided then to tell him a few more things about myself, like the time I fell in love with a hoary old desert tortoise, and a few small details about my love life with Julio.

(I did not tell him of things mi hermano, Raúl, had asked me to keep quiet about, and sworn me to secrecy on our mother's Bible.)

I don't know why I decided to reveal these things to D. I think I wanted to scare him away. Why shouldn't he know what an unsavory person he had decided to marry?

Secretly I hoped he would send me back.

I am not good enough for him. What if he is unable to complete his thesis because of me? What if I ruin his life?

October 1996, Rio Hondo

I had written to Sr. Sarasco to inquire if anyone had heard from my vagrant brother Raúl. I have sent so many letters to our box. Raúl didn't even congratulate me on my marriage. I am worried about him. It has been too long.

No news of Raúl, no news of Julio, Sr. Sarasco sadly reported. But he asked me to send him a story, or a poem, or a description of my life here in the United States. He is starting up a periodical and wants to include something from me!

He was always a big encouragement. I wonder when I will see him again. I think perhaps I will try to call him on the telephone, to have a conversation. I miss his voice, always patiently explaining the grammar and the chemistry. He was my favorite teacher.

So, I must write for him a story, and I must write in español—which is going kind of rusty here. I have a title I like: "Jill with No Jack."

March 1997, Rio Hondo
Dearest Diario,
I know I have neglected you, but well . . . I am older now and have much to concern myself about.

But here is some good news!

Next week we are moving into our own apartment. In San Francisco! Now I can really feel like a wife to David. It has been difficult being so near his family all these months.

His mother, in particular, never lets me forget that David has a brilliant career as a scientist ahead of him . . . as if it were me (not himself!) keeping him from it all these months. I don't know if he was being rebellious, or just lazy.

So now, it is settled. David will finish his studies at the University of California. And I will find a job.

San Francisco is a town I like very much (another saint, of course). We have visited often when house-sitting, in Tiburon, for Damasco's Uncle Bob. A man I most admired, a man who was always kind and respectful to me.

I am glad that we will see more of him now. And though I am told the weather in San Francisco can be cold and wet any time of the year, I am ready for this change.

David and I have had happy times in Rio Hondo with the horses and the sunshine and all the trees, but I am anxious to begin making a real home for us, even if it will be cramped at first. Apartments in San Francisco are very expensive, he says. We will be living off his small stipend, at first.

However, I want to work. I know how to work! I have managed a tiendita grocery and I can plant and cook and sew and write and read . . . reading is one thing I know how to do very well.

Rose Street, San Francisco, March 1998
I love my job. I am making new friends at work. David seems content. He is working hard at his studies, and making progress.

This weekend I finished crocheting a cover for

our bed. (It is always chilly at night here! Nothing like Rio Hondo.)

I used two colors of yarn. I designed a dark half-moon floating in the middle of a light background. Cream-white, like the clouds we view from the rooftop here on Rose Street. I am certain I can hear the ocean, but David says that's impossible. However, we have both heard the fog horns on occasion. Haunting and beautiful. I imagine the large boats floating under the Golden Gate Bridge, way out into the distance.

I have a secret, Dear Diary, that I must keep even from you. It remains to be seen how this new development will turn out. I no longer worry so much about Raúl, he has become distant in my mind. But I worry about David a lot. I don't want him to be harmed in any way, or troubled, or ever to die. I don't want him to quit his studies, or become disappointed with me, in any way. I want to be with him always. He has become so dear to me. It makes me afraid.

I did the dreaming last night, for the first time in a long while.

Dream Diary Five
Esta es mi mente, la reina es cumplidora, cumbre de nada, cariño, espiritu, líbrame, nuevos mundos, antiguos, cuidados, abandonados . . .

Silence! . . . *se necesita ese silencio para crear*

palabras nuevas y sonoras . . .

Ahora. Now it begins. . . .

I am alone. A long sandy stretch of beach before me. My crew has abandoned me . . . or I them. It is impossible to say.

I hear música popular off in the distance. A ladies voice, soothing, intones: "Ninety-five calories never tasted so imported."

A man's voice, self-assured, reports: "Government experts say Vivarin is safe and effective."

I cool my feet in the green-black sea. . . . This is Mexico, the Caribbean edge. I seem to have walked some distance without shoes and I seem to be naked most of the time, though occasionally I am covered with a thin white blouse that reaches to my knees, or I am bare on top with a red cloth wrapped around my waist, which drifts down in back like a bridal train.

A few old friends are here. I see Miguel from grammar school and I wave for him to join me. We were born on the same day. I was secretly in love with Miguel all through those years of my primary education.

And now, sitting beside me, my wrongly dead sister. Beautiful, kind Ysabel. Lost to me so many years ago. She is smiling. She touches my shoulder. I am happy.

Suddenly Miguel takes me up into his arms and is carrying me away. Ysabel seems distressed, she is waving her arms about, calling my name.

. . . but soon she is out of view as Miguel and I find ourselves floating on a raft in the shallow water, staring

at each other, with longing.

"It is a dangerous trip to Honduras," he says.

"I know," I say, nodding, though I had no idea we were headed there.

When he tells me that it might take weeks or more, and that "he is not ready yet," I decide to go ahead alone, join up with the others along the way.

Miguel agrees that would be best. Then he disappears.

Now I am walking with a crowd of strangers. We pass dry salt beds and stagnant lagoons. I have brought along a blanket, a pair of binoculars, a large schoolroom clock, and some bricks neatly stacked, on a chrome suitcase carrier with rubber wheels.

I find myself standing in the central square of a small Mexican town. A voice explains, "This is the place where the two threads meet." I am confused, turning my head this way and that, to locate something I recognize.

A smiling, pudgy boy wearing a tailored, pin-stripe suit and high-heeled shoes comes to my rescue.

"How do you do?" he says in perfect English.

I ask him to help me find the road to Honduras.

He says his grandmother knows, and further, "She will be here soon . . . meanwhile, let me tell you about myself."

He plops down on the bench beside me and begins to chatter. He is from the middle classes, he says, laughing. "And so, I must wear nice clothes even when there is no reason for it."

"Those boys," he points to a group playing marbles in

the dirt, "Those boys can wear rags if they wish to. I envy them." He removes his shoes and begins rubbing his toes.

His grandmother appears beside him, carrying a bag of ice, which she drops in the dust at her grandson's feet.

She is clearly old, but not old-looking, with calm skin and dark far-reaching eyes. She says she was seventy-three when the war in Honduras started. "That was twenty years ago."

I nod politely, though I am astonished at her words.

"I will take you there," she adds, though I hadn't asked.

We ride in her midnight-blue sedan . . . two luxurious banks of seats. I am in back with the grandson. The car is long and sleek. It glides gracefully over the road. There are no knobs or handles anywhere. No mirrors, no headlights, no tail-lights, no chrome. The inside is plush and smooth as a coffin. There are no gauges on the dash, just a long slender reflective surface embedded in purple velvet, with flecks of gold and white. There is enough room inside the car for the universe to collapse and start up again. Which it does, for me, briefly, as she explains that we have met before.

"In San Francisco, don't you remember? You showed me your poetry."

"Poetry?" I am baffled. But then it all comes clear.

I met this same calm-voiced woman on a bus on the way to a photo exhibition. She had been injured in some way. I wanted to help her.

I had showed her a page from my diary. It described

a day in Tiburon, when David was off at the Center. That day, I walked alone to greet the healing plants that grow wild along the road. I spoke with a homeless man sipping coffee from a cup. I met a ten-year-old boy who showed me the fish he had caught. He explained that what looked like sticks floating on the waves were actually the backs of sea lions. I met two firemen with whom I conversed in Spanish. I sat alone on a bench and watched the waves.

It was, in its way, a perfect day. . . .

She tells me that her husband is a hermaphrodite in charge of three male archangels: Animals, Fire, and Metals. She herself is an overseer for three female archangels: Earth, Water, and Plants. Her husband suddenly appears in the seat beside her. A young man of about eighteen.

"Don't be fooled," she warns, "he is even older than I am. And he's both cruel and strong." She smoothes her long white braid.

As we drive, the scene out the windows flickers.

Empty fields, peaks shrouded by moody clouds. A luminous silver-purple, like mercury, reflects an oncoming storm. The road is straight, narrow, rutted, rocky, yet sprinkled with a fine layer of sand. Silkweed and blackbrush dot the hills. Tiny yellow flowers line the embankment. The sky boils with turbulence.

The old grandmother is an excellent driver.

Her grandson, beside me, puffs on a thin brown cigarette. He removes his square-shaped, orange-framed sunglasses. I notice that the left lens is clear, while the right one is dark. Both lenses are cracked.

His cigarette fills the air with a delicious scent. I ask about it.

"Well you see our people made their wealth through the cultivation of vanilla," he exhales a fragrant curl of smoke which he gathers into his fist and tosses out the open window.

"The sheath, the shaft, all in one. Which is why we live so elegantly!"

He tightens a maroon scarf around his neck as the air turns suddenly cold.

We arrive at the edge of the churning waters. A thread of light penetrates the dark sky. Rough, broken waves strike the shoreline.

The boy says, "Don't worry, this isn't deep water. Just the bay."

I have heard those words before. . . .

A group has gathered at water's edge. Some are strangers . . . a few I recognize. Familiar faces from the swimming hole back in Mexico.

But where is Miguel, and Ysabel? Where is Julio?

And what about David? My Damasco. Wasn't he supposed to join me?

A little girl spins her arms in circles like a pinwheel. She rides on the back of her strong, youthful brother. A leering old man with blackened teeth shouts to the crowd: "An odd one, isn't she? Reminds me of a dirty old bat."

Just then, a large bat flies overhead, dropping seed.

A crescent moon floats above the darkening hills. It is impossible to say whether it is day or night. I wonder why the air feels so cold since I know we must be close to the equator.

Far away, balanced in the waves, an enormous concrete ship drops its anchor. A small fiber-glass boat is docked on the algae-rich rocks . . . lacy drapes of seaweed dangle from the oars.

The lovely old grandmother gestures toward the row boat. I strain to hear what she is saying. . . .

Then, as the wind changes, I hear her voice as clearly as if she lived inside me:

"Travel east against the sun. You will meet your potencia. Do not hesitate. You will know what to do. Go!"

"But why must I go?"

"I don't know. I am only a messenger."

While I am struggling into the boat, she shouts:

"Wait! I have something to give you."

She hands me a sewn ubre, filled with seeds or pearls. She utters the words:

"Keep this with you always. For now, do not share with anyone."

I nod in assent. I unmoor the boat. I row and row and row and row as fast as I can, then, glancing back, I see she is gone. Even the shore has disappeared.

The enormous waves seem to be made of molten metals, copper, silver, iron, and lead. The ship's horn sounds its final call. . . .

[diary ends]

1998–1999 Notebooks: David Ambrose Gentry

Begin again. Dismembered. Complexity circumscribes but does not explain. There are *no reasons* for some things.

Eons have passed since her death. I've lost the thread.

SIN is my middle name. It is a sin to receive more than you deserve. I didn't deserve Colibri. Wrong of me. To bring her here.

I sit with a pencil and a bottle. I take a sip from the bottle. I move the pencil over paper. What I write about is death. My life infused with thoughts of her death. Who caused it and why? I suspect everyone, my parents, her colleagues, her brother, the guy who works at the grocery store down the street. Even myself.

Ninety percent of the cells in our bodies are bacteria. The dot on this "i" could be filled with millions of them. Are we even ten percent human? What is "human" anyway?

We have identified less than one percent of the organisms on our planet. The bulk of life is invisible. Most is in the sea. Micro-organisms.

Or in psychology. Buried deep.

I return to these notebooks, hers and mine, for a clue or direction.

— 10.2.98 S.I.N.

A book in my hand contains thirty-three myths written in a dialect of Chinook known only to three persons at the time the research was undertaken. 1890.

The territory of the now-dead language once extended from Astoria along the Columbia River. As far as Mount Rainier.

Memorize lists. Keep the mind flowing:

Aleut, Alsea, anger is useless, Aranama, Assyrian, Atakapa, Biloxi, Bontoc-Irogot, burdensome I am to myself and everyone else, Castellana, Celtic, Chaldean, chastising is worthless, Chitimacha, Chocktaw, Coalhuilteco, Cotoname, Cree, Dakota, devoted I was to her but it didn't help, Etruscan, Goajira, Guarani, Heve, heaven has no compassion, Hidatsa, Karankawa, Kinkolith, Kongo, Lala, larlept a word she used in love-making, Luganda, Malabar, Malay, Maori, my own true love is gone how do I go on, Mpongwe, Natick, Nazi, Nootka, Ofo, only if I had found her sooner maybe she would be alive, Onondaga, Otchipwe, Paey, Pennsylvania Dutch, Ronga, Samia, Samarita, Samoan, she sensed her own death in a dream, Sissarro, Slavonic, Sumerian, Tagalog, Tarasca, Tsimshian, Tzotzil, Ulawa, Voltaic, volumes of the unknown weigh on me, Welsh, Yemeni, Zande, end it all here.

Can't recall how to enjoy any of my former pleasures. Walking on the beach brings on an

attack of anxiety. Don't talk much to anyone about where we / I / he are or what he / I / we am doing.
— 11.2.98 NAMING

Watchtower lady left two pamphlets under my door. One titled: "You Can Meet the Challenge of Youth."

I don't think so. Not yet twenty-five and already ruined.

The second one reads: "Death, Is It Really the End? Also, How Can I Avoid Pornography?"

Weeks after Colibri's death, I began a strange practice. I picked up women. Lonely types you find by themselves in bars. I'd try to get drunk. Invite the woman back to the apartment. Try to get her to fuck my brains out. A couple of times it almost worked.

I was on the brink of something. Would see things clearly for a moment.

With one woman the effect lasted days.

I wasn't crude or unkind to them. But they seemed frightened at times. I sobered up. Saw each one home, or into a cab, or wherever she wanted to go. Most were divorced. Some, maybe, considering prostitution as a career. I gave money on impulse a few times.

I was surprised how easy it was to get them to go with me. And how easy to get rid of them afterwards. Never saw any of them again.

I can't really understand how it got going. But perhaps I do. A psychotherapist told me I blamed myself for Colibri's death. This crude sex was a form of self-punishment.

I didn't get any diseases. Been lucky in some ways. Had sex with a dozen women during a period of four weeks. As suddenly as the urge started, it ended.

Once, I told Colibri my vision of the end of nature. All that was left was a square-mile-fenced-off piece of land, which the ants had taken over. She said it meant I was afraid of death and wanted to take everyone along with me. She said that's what men want deep inside. That's why we scrape and rape and poison and pollute the earth.

At the time, I told her she was being mean. It was rare for her to be so brutally honest.

— 2.19.99 RELATIONS

Some say the leaves of basil cure grief. Others say basil can kill. A woman today at the grocery told me to try the "blessed herb" valerian for a mindless sleep.

I remember Colibri telling me that a person could mourn for "thirteen moons" but then must cease all mourning. We were visiting the turtle preserves at Mazunté. We watched a lonely turtle circling in the sand. Lost among the monolithic rocks that were encrusted with bird shit.

El número trece era muy significante, I hear C. saying.

Trece las lunas de un año solar, y trece menstruaciones. . . .

It will be one year this week. I've been unable to continue my studies. I'm a burden to my family. To society. Old pal John calls often. Leaves probing messages. Jack sends urgent notes about returning to our research. He's got a wife and kids to feed. Uncle Bob sends kind letters on his fine stationary. Mom thinks all will be solved if I just come back home for a while.

I regret that I drifted from them.

With C. gone, I don't have anything to offer.

I've just moved from the apartment C. and I shared, into a small room, in a dilapidated building. I must do something. I don't know what it is.
— March 1999 RELATIONS

At first I decided to devote my life to finding her killer. The police were useless. The investigation went nowhere. No witnesses. No motive. She wasn't raped or robbed. Her bag had spilled and the scent of nutmeg filled the air. No fingerprints, no weapon, no clues.

I was inside at the time. Watching, on the news, the great fire at Mortem Fendano Botanical Library. My mind was consumed with the loss of vast stores of irreplaceable biological materials, while the love of my life was beaten to death on our doorstep.

Why did she of all people have to meet such a fate?

Colibri was an innocent. She had no enemies. Few can say that about themselves.

Her death makes no sense. I wish I could believe in something.

Against all reason, I hope there is some kind of afterlife. That her presence or her spirit continue to exist. That thoughts can somehow reach her. I was watching TV. Colibri had gone out to pick up some missing ingredient for dinner. She was always very particular about things.

Arson was suspected in the great fire. Use of unusual plasma explosives. The Library contained the most comprehensive collection of generative plant material in the Western Hemisphere. Seeds, buds, cuttings, pollen, spores, from endangered or extinct species worldwide. Our tickets to Bogotá in my pocket. We were planning to fly the following week. A one-year stipend working in recovery of DNA sequencing. The UCSD grant had finally come through, after numerous bureaucratic delays.

I didn't hear her scream. She was dead when I got there. On the steps in the doorway to our apartment building. Did a neighbor ring the bell? Difficult to remember now. Reason eclipsed by grief.

No last words. The pain she must have felt. Not reflected in her face. Her face wore its familiar expression of acceptance.

I was wrong to bring her to the United States. I thought I could help her but I was only being selfish. Her life in Mexico wasn't ideal. Maybe she would be alive today if she had stayed. If I had left her alone.

I'm convinced now of the great ugliness of human beings. No one visits my twelve-by-twelve-foot room. I share a bathroom and a kitchen with seven others. Most of them Chinese immigrants. For the past few months I've been lying to Mom. Told her I've got a nice rooftop apartment. She and Clive are in the Caribbean. My heart is frozen.

— 4.12.99 RELATIONS

Items found in C.'s closet after her death:
1. manila envelope full of letters: mostly her mother's old letters, and some from Julio (a few of the early post cards I had sent her)
2. embroidered handkerchief with a spot of blood (analysis proved C.'s DNA, probably from her first menses)
3. "mirror" of polished obsidian (I knew about that, it scared me)
4. small "tanka" of seated deities inside a flaming circle, hand-painted on cloth, wrapped in paper

in a brown mailing tube, postmarked "Juárez 2.29.98," no return address (why hadn't I seen this when it arrived?)

5. C.'s hand-written diaries in plain black "essay" books, wrapped in a lime green scarf, which features the sites of San Francisco: Great Highway, Fisherman's Wharf, Golden Gate, Coit Tower (I gave that scarf to her)

6. beat-up army cap embroidered with the letters "GS" (I've seen that before)

7. an unmarked packet of seeds

I turned all of this over to the investigative team. (Kept back a sample of the seeds, and some of her medicinal dried flowers.) They made copies of the letters and diaries and returned the originals to me. The cap and the cloth painting held the most potential. Juárez post office designation.

What do the letters on the cap stand for?

Chief investigator Jim Reed and his protegé, Jane May, met with me several times. Their team scoured the neighborhood. Questioned everyone. Pursued all leads. Nothing. The only clues I had were those items you, C., had hidden from me at the back of your closet, in a *malinalli* grass basket.

The letters from Julio hurt. I suspected him until I read the letters again.

I was disturbed by the carved wooden angel you kept on a shelf above our bed. It was from

Julio, you said. And that hardback book you were reading. Something about "Telementation." One time I saw you polishing the obsidian mirror but I never saw you using it.

I took the painting on cloth to an appraiser to have it assessed. They said it was of a Tibetan deity. Green Tara. Mid-20th century. One woman hinted it might have come from the collection of a man in the city who'd recently died. Murdered with one of his own possessions. A severe alcoholic who kept scanty records.

She assured me that the *tanka* was a fairly common one and "not museum quality." They did, however, offer me, on the spot, a thousand dollars in cash, which I refused.

I didn't tell them that the painting belonged to you, Colibri, and that you had been murdered, too.

Reported all this and much superfluous information to Inspector Reed.

Tried in vain to reach your "family." What was left of it. Numerous letters to Raúl at your Oaxaca Post Box. And letters to your teacher, Sr. Sarasco.
— 5.18.99 RELATIONS

Started a new regime. Two or three times a week I ride BART to the sperm bank in Berkeley. To deposit my seed. I've been thoroughly and exhaustively tested. Apparently, I'm a rare breed these days. High sperm count, the right amount of fluid. Resistance to common viruses, which can cause problems for infants. STDs, HIV and HEP repeatedly tested—in the negative. They're going to get a maximum of ten pregnancies out of me before they ax me. Generally it's five live births, each with an option for another, should the mother want two.

I asked, why only ten, and the director said they don't want to "bias the gene pool."

The only way I can ejaculate is to think about the times with C. I know that's probably unhealthy, but I can't do it any other way.

At least I'm good for something.

— 7.28.99 S.I.N.

I have to do something to find your killer, C. The investigators concluded it was not the work of a professional. You weren't robbed. You weren't violated. Your purse had dropped and spilled. Coroner reported cause of death as "cerebral concussion resulting in sudden and massive hemorrhage."

Detective Reed defined it as "a fall onto stone steps in response to an attack by an unknown assailant."

Maybe there was no intention to murder? Rob or rape maybe, bad enough. But when you fell so hard, your assailant bolted.

Or—this is my nightmare—you tripped and

fell in horror, recognizing the man.

There were contusions on the scalp but the fatal bleeding was internal.

For months I believed that your brother Raúl was the key to your death. I didn't know where to begin to search. I tried the police, U.S. immigration, and Mexican authorities.

Pestered Uncle Bob to use his State Department contacts.

What I didn't do was go to Oaxaca.

I was afraid—not for my life—but afraid of how I would feel in the places where we met and fell in love.

Nothing can bring you back.

I remember the time we went to the Del Mar horse track, outside San Diego. Near the stables, you saw a groom you recognized. Hauling a bale of hay.

"It's him," you whispered.

"Who?"

You shook your head.

"A guy from Chihuahua . . . one of my brother's buddies."

I suggested you talk to him. Ask him about Raúl.

"No!" you begged, "*Por favor.* Let it go. Raúl is legend now. I cannot think I will ever see him again."

I was certain you knew more than you were

willing to say.

On the way home, as we passed through orange groves ignited by the setting sun, you explained how Mexican grooms and their horses have a special love affair.

"That's why the grooms are so successful and why their horses always win. The grooms don't marry, they don't care much for girlfriends or having children. Horses are everything to them."
— 8.16.99 S.I.N.

The psychotherapist Mom sent me to see—after C.'s death—signed me up for everything. He said that my disorientation would pass in time. But for now I needed all the help I could get.

I use food stamps at the Pine Street Grocery. Go to the post office to pick up my SSI check: "Saviors of the Sane and Insane," as John describes it. Ride the bus with my lifetime pass. Try to feel something for the other sad-looking ones like myself.

I liked our little apartment. Up on the roof we could watch the sun drop toward the ocean. We lived on an alley called Rose Street. Nearby, yes, were "the projects." Our block had a nice park with iron benches. Birds of paradise and sycamore trees.

Most days I dropped C. off at work and picked her up on my way back from UCB. I feel the same about her now, only the feelings have grown stronger.

Why did you hide things from me, C.?

Was it to protect your brother or Julio or someone else?

Was it to protect me, or yourself?

Secrets. In determining that there had been "no criminal sexual contact" the coroner discovered that you were carrying an embryo.

Five or six weeks at most.

There was no way of saving the baby or you.

How could I know?

How could I not know?

—10.25.99 S.I.N.

2000 Notebooks: David Ambrose Gentry

Bad weekend. Completely unbalanced.

Failed plans for killing self even though I'd managed to procure enough prescription reds from a friend. Dusted off my Smith & Wesson. A present from dear Dad on my fourteenth birthday.

Six-shot, double-action revolver. Forty-four magnum cartridge. Walnut grip. Like in Taxi Driver.

Fourteen. That was the year Dad taught me to shoot. Target practice was his idea of a birthday gift. He also offered to take me to a "woman in the service industry." As his father had done for him.

I said, "Dad, guys don't have to pay for it anymore."

Remembered all this when I pulled out the gun from the box under my desk. Familiar oiled steel smell.

Back when I was a boy, I wanted to shoot something. Anything. (Probably, in retrospect, I really wanted to shoot Dad.) Shot a squirrel and a couple of sparrows. Mom locked the gun away. That was the end of my shooting spree.

Stuff in the box I had completely forgotten. Stock certificates from Dad's corporation: Hexion Finance Group. Been getting small dividends regularly, but didn't realize I had the actual certificates.

Dad always wore a tie. Neatly barbered hair. Dignified. Didn't know how to relax. Except, maybe, with his girlfriends. I saw him three or four times a year after he and Mom split up. Didn't look forward to those meetings. We had nothing to talk about.

He died just before I started college. He would have been disappointed. Wanted me to go to a biz school. Like Stanford. His Alma Mater. I was always interested in science. In nature. Thought I might end up a veterinarian. Had to have pets. Snakes, lizards, birds. And dogs, of course.

No cats. Dad hated cats.

Originally I'd intended to jump from the Golden Gate Bridge. Fantasy. Didn't have enough energy to get myself there. As backup, in case I couldn't pull the trigger, went to the corner liquor and bought a fifth of Jack Daniels. Thinking I'd wash down the pills with that. Put a plastic bag over my head.

Imagined someone phoning police. People in this building mostly speak Chinese. Guess the police would make the call to Mom. Or the hospital staff if I'd botched it. She'd wail. She'd tear at her hair and sob, "Why? Why? Why?!"

Clive would comfort her. She'd get over it. Eventually. Still, I know it's a cruel thing to do.

They might not discover my body for a while. This whole place already smells rank with the unwashed obese woman next door and the bum who accidentally pisses on the stairs. The garbage in our shared kitchenette.

I'd have to leave some kind of note. "Gone to join my true love."

It all seemed absurd.

Easier to drink the whiskey and turn on the TV. A death-in-life experience, anyway. Decided, instead, to make myself useful in some way.

C. used to say: *Everyone dies. If they are lucky, they leave behind a thing or two of value, to be incorporated into others.*

— I.20.2000 S.I.N.

Meditating and maintaining my "purity." Sperm bank twice a week. Talked at length with the receptionist. Interesting woman. Asks a lot of questions. Her name is G:

"G-E-E as in bee or just G or G with a period?" I asked.

"Just G," she said.

Found myself telling her about a group meeting I recently attended. People seeking a life-long commitment to celibacy.

You'd think they'd all be homely. Not so. Interesting, attractive people. Various ages and persuasions. More men than women, surprisingly. Many of the women have experienced abuse and/or incest. A few are clinically frigid or suffer from some incurable medical condition.

One beautiful young Korean woman confessed she'd become addicted to sex after being molested, for years, by her uncle. Said it was ruining her life.

After laboring over the four-page questionnaire (detailing our work interests, hobbies, entertainment choices, pets, and religious views) we discussed what we want from a relationship:

Sharing a house, sharing a life, occasional companionship?

I listed my occupation as "yogi"—god knows why. That got a few laughs and raised eyebrows.

"What *is* a yogi?" a middle-aged woman asked.

"One who practices a technique to discipline the mind and body and liberate the soul."

Big bald guy said, "And what is the soul?"

That set the group off.

Kissing and cuddling are high on the group's "TO DO" list, orgasm with another is out. Too much emotional risk.

— 2.2.2000 RELATIONS

The sperm bank founder (attractive dyke, Cyrene) said the building we are in was once a mortuary. Crematorium still out back. Dead bodies. Living sperm. She talked about Spallanzani's experiments freezing sperm. Way back in 1776.

Cyrene is well-known as the inventor of an organic "sponge" used as sperm or germ barrier.

"Superclays will be used in the future," she told me.

"We might ingest them like vitamins. Or, they could be implanted in the body, functioning like cysts, to remove toxins."

I was reminded of *Arabidopsis thaliana.* Simple mustard. Like the one that eats up lead. The first to release its genetic blueprint for the benefit of humankind. Lots of DNA mapping has been done since then. Eventually we may grow synthetic organisms to cure all our ills. . . .

Thalamus = inner chamber, marriage bed.

They said there was irreparable damage to C.'s thalamus. The attack, the fall, the hemorrhage. I saw the X-rays. The beautiful flower of Colibri's mind displayed in cross-section.

— 2.12.00 NAMING

Guy on TV. Huge body. A completely scar-encrusted face. Viet Nam vet. They did their best to reconstruct his features. Wasn't much to work with. Hard to see his nose. Ragged slits for eyes. Scar tissue everywhere. He wore an enormous pale grey suit. Spoke his testimonial:

I didn't know what hit me. I was engulfed by flames. My face was on my boots. I could see my heart beating in my chest. My back was on fire, skin dripping off my arms. My hands were severed in half. I didn't know what to do.

Suddenly I felt the presence of The Lord like a soothing breeze all around me. And the pain was gone. I prayed to Jesus, then and there. My father always said that God never deserts the disabled. . . . Why didn't I pray to say Bud, or Harry, or Mo? Because Bud, and Harry, and Mo didn't die for me on the cross, that's why!

I looked so-o-o bad. You think I'm bad now but I really looked bad then. I looked so bad the doctor told me to take my veteran's loan and buy some land and live on it with my wife. Let her go to town, let her do the shopping. Don't—the doc insisted—put yourself in the position of suffering a social life.

Well now look at me! Here I am on TV. Thirty years later. . . .

You see, Jesus didn't desert me. He told me to go out there and tell my story. He told me to inspire others to sacrifice, to give themselves to Christ. I did that and he gave my life meaning.

I believed the guy. Cried my fucking eyes out.
— 3.4.2000 RELATIONS

Am I paranoid? Past few days I've noticed a guy standing across the street, between the potted trees. He seems to be looking at my window. Dark, hooded jacket. When I go out, he isn't there.

And someone has been messing with my mail. It's all been opened or crushed. Even the weekly posts from Mom and Clive.

Called Detective Reed. Got a return call from his associate, Jane May.

The sound of her voice did something to me. Confident, reassuring. She said she'd look into it and get back to me right away.

Tomorrow, two years will have passed, and nothing has been revealed.
— 3.20.2000 RELATIONS

Weeks alone in my study. Advances in meditation. Gaining access to a deeper part of my mind. Had to stop today. Overcome by sadness. This time it came up from my diaphragm and rippled through my chest like a freight train. I went to the window, threw open the shade and was inundated by the daylight world.

Watched a man on the street below scrounging through trash. He found something he liked. Lucky man.

My books, my computer, my tooth brush, a single sock in the corner. All pervaded by sadness.

Across the street, trees in redwood boxes. Leaves shaking in the wind. Male mulberry trees. Never to blossom or bear fruit. Sterile trees planted throughout the city, "To keep the sidewalks clean."

Neighbor hung up a wind chime on the fire escape. Poignant notes bless my mood. *To meditate is to transcend time. It is only when the mind transcends time that truth ceases to be an abstraction.*—Words of Krishnamurti, Monroe's mentor.

C. and I spent ecstatic hours at Ocean Beach. One time, I ignored the ocean to read an SFI bulletin. She poked me in the arm, exasperated.

David, you are here now! Look at the sky, look at those waves. . . . Why are you wanting to be some other where?

Black fly crawling up the glass attracts my attention.

Across the Bay, hills stable and consistent.

Colibri loved Julio. Then she loved me. Maybe he came back to curse her. To kill her. No. My reason is in control for a moment. Anyone she loved so much would not do such a thing.

Chief investigator Reed told me to "let it be."

He pointed to the projects.

"Don't keep looking for a reason. An angry man walked out onto the streets and encountered your sweetheart. There's no sense looking any farther. We've tried everything."

He sighed. Resting his hand on my shoulder briefly. He confessed that his own daughter had been kidnapped when she was quite young.

"She never got over it."

The theory preferred by the homicide team is

that someone, most likely a thief, scared Colibri. She started to scream. She was assaulted and fell, hitting her head. The fall is what actually killed her.

She died on our doorsteps, while I was inside. Oblivious. That's the part I can't wrap my mind around.

I lie on my futon. My throat gripped in spasms of despair.

Rays of sunlight penetrate the air. I hear the old man clomping his way up the stairs. He'll cough a few times and stumble his way down the hall to his door.

Was he ever in love? Did he have youthful hopes and dreams?

What is sin, David?

Something that leads you away from the truth of your own nature.

Do you remember the name of this yellow flower?

Alone in my study. Practice the meditation. Inundated by the glaring daylight world. Crawling up the glass. Hills of loss. Brassy rays of sunlight. Relieved of hopes and dreams.

— 3.23.2000 S.I.N.

G at sperm bank asked me to write down one of my dreams. She's involved in a study based on people who frequent the clinic.

I told her I don't remember my dreams. A lie.

They say I'm up to nine. Already seven live births, with two "options." Director tells me I'm one of their "specials." More women choose me from the files than they can allow. How could that possibly be? Guess I look good on paper. Or, the other guys are real losers.

Can't decide if I am an egomaniac or just a regular guy. Probably both. Why would I want to propagate myself or my species?

I need to give life to something.

From the literature:

SPERM DONOR REQUIREMENTS

1. *Thorough history spanning three generations of family members.* [My father's heart attack and my fascist, Sicilian, drunkard Grandpa didn't phase them.]

2. *Numerous semen samples under varied conditions to evaluate: motility, sperm count, and morphology. Note: it's acceptable for up to 40% of sperm to be abnormally shaped—i.e., two-tails, two-heads [!?!], small head, large head, asymmetry.*

3. *Initial and ongoing exhaustive physical/mental examinations.* [Hard to believe I've passed that with flying colors.]

Note: Only cryo-preserved semen is used, not fresh. If you plan your visit around your fertile time, we can perform the insemination. Or arrangements can be made to ship the specimens directly to your home or office.

What's that, Sally, fresh lobster from Maine?

No, I'm afraid it's only my sperm donation. Guess I'll need the afternoon off . . . ha-ha-hah!

The clinic's founder built her life around the concept that reproduction should be separated from sex. *The choice to reproduce, or not reproduce, should be available to all, based on informed consent. It must become a conscious act, not the by-product of a whimsical or mindless encounter.*

Now, that's a radical idea!

Weirdly, some abstinence is required. Forty-eight hours is the minimal interval it takes to replenish sperm. However, if abstinence continues for several weeks, there is likely to be an accumulation of aging and dead sperm in the ejaculate.

Abstinence does not make the sperm grow stronger.

It's in the literature. No kidding.

What do they do with all the unused seed? Feed it to rats in biological experiments? Probably.

— 4.18.2000 S.I.N.

Ran into Detective Jane May. Literally ran right into her. Buying apricots at a fruit stand. Wasn't even sure I knew what she looked like. But she called out my name and I recognized her voice.

Streaked hair blowing across red-framed

sunglasses. Short plaid skirt. Green striped tights. Had only seen her a few times during the interrogations. Always before she was modestly dressed. Her hair tied back neatly.

This was a real surprise. . . .

She assured me that she was just about to call me. To let me know that Chief Inspector Reed would soon retire and she would be taking over the case.

I shook her hand. Said I was pleased.

Last night, oddly erotic dream of her. Meeting near the fish tanks in a pet store. She wore long white earrings made of origami paper cranes. We were both interested in the little ceramic castles they put into fish bowls. (What are they for? To make the fish feel at home?)

In the dream, I noticed a large diamond ring at the bottom of one tank. I reached in and fished it out for her. She smiled as she put the ring on her finger. Suddenly, it became way too large and heavy. Encrusted with barnacles.

Maybe I should tell that one to G.

I'm determined to try to remain celibate for a time. I knew that if I started writing in these notebooks again, I would run the risk of encountering my atrophied emotional self. Ah well, here it is in all its gory glory.

Monroe speaks to me from books and audio recordings: *The law of levity is as real as the law of gravity. Levity has everything to do with release from attachment to self-importance.*

Recently, I've been wondering about the immigration authorities. There was a bureaucratic tangle back when I tried to get C's green card.

That's why we had decided the best plan was to go ahead and get married. At first they didn't believe she was eighteen. Even though she had her passport and work papers. Sending for birth records was a farce.

Maybe someone at immigration is involved in the crime network Raúl is part of? Maybe someone wanted information from C., and she couldn't give it. Or wouldn't. Or maybe she did.

Was she protecting her brother? Or some other lover? Or, was she in on it? Whatever it was. Because of Raúl?

Re-reading her diaries now.

Devotion to familia is so strong in her world.

The homicide team has never cleared *me* of suspicion. It could be their men watching me. Dark hooded jacket. SUV. Always felt Inspector Reed didn't entirely trust me. Maybe just my sick imagination.

Monroe: *The stuff of the soul consists of two eternally conflicting elements: "love" and "malice." It is love that allows us to have compassion for other living things. It is malice that causes the separation between human beings and nature, between humans and one another.*

— 10 pm 4.27.2000 S.I.N.

An enormously overweight woman with some kind of skin disease lives in the room next to mine. An odor from her room creeps in under my door. Some kind of incense or body cream.

Sometimes I hear her sobbing at night.

I wish I could do something for her.

I wish I could help that one pathetic, noble, human being.

Funny thing is, as I write this, I feel closer to her than to anyone else in the world.

— 5.12.2000 RELATIONS

Unbelievable! I return with groceries. Find the door wide open. Everything turned upside-down, inside-out. Jesus Christ! What's missing?

My computer is gone. CD player. Books in complete chaos. Drawers pulled out and contents heaped on the floor. Cardboard boxes of printer paper and cartridges of ink ripped open.

Somebody obviously looking for something. What?

Money? Checkbook still here.

Bag of weed and pipe are gone. Figures.

Can't find Colibri's seeds and the dried flowers I kept back from "evidence" given to the homicide team. Hm-m-m. The pillow of dill, also gone. Dropper bottles of herbal remedies, samples from the natural foods store, gone. What kind of thieves are these? Drug abusers or sophisticated investigators? They had to work fast because I was gone little over an hour.

My notebooks are here. Colibri's diaries as well. Amazing. Still under the desk along with my (now worthless) University papers.

Looks like they came in through the window, by the fire escape. I knocked on the door of the woman next door and she kindly answered all my questions. But she didn't have any answers.

No one here heard anything or saw anyone.

Lots of noise night and day with the fire department across the street. And the warehouses. And all the liquor store activity.

I think I'm finally able to consider moving out of this place.

Called Detective Reed's office. Reed and Jane May were out. Reed called back from his cell phone and told me two officers were on their way. They showed up and did some fancy stuff. Including fingerprinting. Nothing of course. Not encouraging. Surprised at the level of chaos. Not your typical smash and grab.

They busted open Colibri's urn. Her ashes on the floor. That just about did me in.

Same fucked-up day! Jane May just phoned to let me know that a man who fit the description of Raúl—carrying I.D. papers to back it—had just been stabbed in the Mission Street BART station.

She wondered if, since I had met Raúl [only once in Mexico] would I agree to identify the body.

I said, "No. I don't think so." I was filled with rage.

What was Raúl doing in San Francisco? How long had he been here? Was he in contact with C. at the time of her death? I knew I couldn't be certain it was Raúl, but if it was Raúl, I didn't want to see the stinking bastard's face.

Distinct lengthy pause on the line.

I know I'm still under suspicion. Maybe now the Department suspects me of Raúl's murder too. Fucking shit. Changed my tune.

"Okay, I'll come."

Distinct sigh of relief on her end.

We are to meet at 9 pm in the city morgue.

— 6.23.00 NAMING

It's him. It *was* him, is the way to say it. Smaller than I remembered. Younger too. Creamy brown skin, just like Colibri's. Something about the mouth. Same smooth distinctive lips. Same patient, accepting expression.

Frightening, for me, how physically alike they were. Even with his beard and broader cheeks.

Colibri was loyal to her brother. She worried about him, she missed him, she said. At least she didn't have to suffer this.

Though I'd always hated him, often suspected

him, blamed him for Colibri's troubles, even possibly her death, I couldn't bring myself to hate him now.

At one time, just after her death, if I'd been able to find him, I might have killed him myself. Someone did it for me. Does one death cancel out the other? No. Never.

Twisted damaged fingers. "Fire burns?" Jane May asked the coroner. He nodded. "Looks to be several years back."

Cause of death: knife wound to the heart. Somebody knew exactly where to insert the blade. And quickly.

"No struggle," coroner said. "He died on the spot."

Any evidence? Anything suspicious he carried with him?

Passport, a little cash, key to a locker or deposit box. No gun. No weapon of any kind? Some sort of asthma inhaler. Chemical analysis pending.

Jane May says the team will get right on it.

Photo in wallet of Colibri. Age twelve, thirteen, maybe. Her shyly smiling innocence. That's a knife to the heart.

Driver's license issued in New Mexico, less than a year ago. Doesn't prove, or disprove, anything.

+++

As we were leaving, Jane May thanked me for coming. And then, with obvious hesitation, asked if the "pharmacological investigator" had contacted me yet.

I had no idea what she was talking about.

She explained that an investigator hired by Pharmco Industries had inquired about Colibri's case, in connection with the Mortem Fendano botanical fire, which occurred on the night of her death.

I asked what kind of connection could there be?

She wasn't able to go into detail "just now" but promised to keep in touch.

I thanked her. She took my hand in both of hers, looked me in the eyes.

"Take care," she said.

Two days later I received this letter. Registered mail. Completely screwed my view of everything.

6.23.2000
Vida Montoya
One International Plaza, Suite 315
Pharmco Industries, Inc.
Middletown, IL

Mr. David Ambrose Gentry,
I have been employed by Pharmco Industries for the past two years to investigate claims made by a competing pharmacological subsidiary—hereafter referred to as "X-Corp." I am a practicing lawyer with a background in investigative journalism.

I'm writing to ask for your assistance with our research into circumstances surrounding the fire at Mortem Fendano Botanical Library in Bogotá, Columbia, on the evening of March 21, 1998.

X-Corp has filed claims that Pharmco illegally attempted to patent certain biological samples originally stored within the repository. Pharmco has been in the process of isolating chemical compounds believed to have therapeutic effects: specifically, analgesic, anti-inflammatory, and pain relieving.

Prior to the fire, a break-in had occurred and samples of rare species from mountainous regions of Western Mexico were found missing.

We have no evidence of a direct connection between

the fire and your wife's death. However, during the initial murder investigation, articles handed over to the FBI belonging to your deceased wife, María Cuerno y Saeta, included a sample of seeds, which was later sent to a Pharmco-affiliated laboratory for analysis.

Those seeds contained a highly specialized chemical formulation, which is the product of sophisticated hybridization. When Pharmco filed for a copyright/patent on this particular chemical signature, X-Corp claimed that they had discovered it first.

I'm sorry to bother you with these details on such a sensitive matter. However, it would be most efficacious, and to your advantage, to please answer the following questions:

1) Are you now, or were you or your wife at any time in the past, in the employ of a pharmaceutical agent or researcher?

2) How did those seeds get into your wife's possession?

3) Do you have any information about the activities and companions of your wife's brother Raúl Cuerno y Saeta?

We are hoping to clear up these questions, as soon as possible, with your cooperation. We are hoping that it will not be necessary to subpoena you, in the event that these claims made by X-Corp come to trial.

I am grateful for your patience and attention to this matter. Please accept my deepest sympathies for the death of your wife.

I would appreciate it if you would write back to me right away. Send your answers registered mail, with your signature, and we will reimburse you for your time and expenses.

Sincere regards,
Vida Montoya, Ph.D., LL.M.

Jesus H. Christ! How incredibly disturbing. How could I have been unaware of something as big as this?

I sat down and wrote back to Montoya on the spot. Thinking, now, about the fact that Colibri and I were scheduled to work at the Library as a team: That particular gig was suggested by one of my profs. Who was *he* working for? C. was very excited about it. Was Raúl connected, in some way, to Pharmco or "X-Corp"? Everything has expanded, exponentially, for me.

These are my honest answers to Montoya's questions:
1) I am not and my wife was not, as far as I know,

ever employed by a pharmaceutical agent or researcher. She worked in the UCSF Biology Deptartment, as a secretary. Please contact them directly if you have further questions.
[Wondering about the cocky guy who hung around her desk. Maybe he knew something, maybe he betrayed her?]

2) I have absolutely no idea how Colibri got the seeds, and no way of finding out, except to say that she knew a lot about the plants in her area, and she probably gathered those seeds herself. She learned many things about plants from her gradmother, who is also deceased.
[I hope I haven't said too much here.]

3) Raúl was in with some rough guys back in Mexico. Colibri had no direct contact with him here, that I know of.
[Didn't say to Ms. Montoya—wish I had—that in my humble opinion no pharmco-titan deserves a copyright or claim on any plant material indigenous to any peoples, regions, or locales on this planet. Hopefully figure out how to spell that out later.]
— 6.27.00 NAMING

Received an almost instant response:
Montoya's letter thanked me for my cooperation

and reiterated that there is no evidence of a connection between C.'s death and the fire, but that the ongoing investigation into the cause of the fire revealed that DNA strains contained in a high-security vault had been tampered with, and an entire area under cultivation, not specifically invaded by the fire, had been removed.

She said they were trying to confirm a link to members of an international "DNA-copyright mafia." Seed banks worldwide have experienced similar disturbing disappearances of vital materials. She had been informed of the recent death of Raúl, and cited his death as a possible connection. She finished her letter with this:

"Please know that though we are keeping these files secure, they are open to scrutiny by the investigative authorities. If any evidence turns up concerning your wife's murder, we will let you know immediately."

— 6.29.00 NAMING

Started my own research. BIOPIRACY MAGAZINE: *Pharmaceutical firms and biotech companies are approaching existing botanical repositories to buy up samples of unique tropical species. This is a clear violation of the spirit—if not the law—of the Convention on Biological Diversity. The rights of farmers and indigenous peoples are being bypassed by corporate deals that make a mockery of the CBD's fundamental principles. These corporations are doing so with the purpose of isolating genes and the proteins they express in order to seek exclusive patents for profit maximization.*

The chief prosecutor for the Brazilian State of Amazonia, who opened an inquiry into biopiracy in 1997, estimates that about 20,000 individual plant samples are illegally removed from the country every year. Scientific laboratories generally receive samples and information from third parties. . . .
— 7.1.00 RELATIONS

Detective Jane called. I was relieved to hear her voice again.

We met yesterday at a favorite café. French roast coffee, chocolate croissants. Discussed Raúl's case. And the implications of the Pharmco letter—with its "indirect threat" to me, as Jane described it. She has a background in law. Came to homicide from that direction, rather than from police work.

Her voice is calm, warm, soothing. She's very appealing physically, with sparkling blue-grey eyes. Maybe a few years older than I am. I noticed a small sharp scar on her left cheek, near her mouth.

I got up for refills and there, on the wall, was the kind of tee-shirt I had given Colibri one Valentine's day. Girly, red, with the formula for caffeine, $C_8H_{10}N_4O_2$, printed in black on the back.

C. thought it funny.

"There they are again, those archangels of the universe, C, H, N, O," she said.

C. and I came here a lot. She always ordered hot chocolate. Even though, she repeatedly assured me, it didn't compare to the cacao back home. Grey-haired Italian who runs the place always called her "bella bella señorita." He layered her cocoa with extra whipped cream and shavings of nutmeg.

Jane asked me a lot of questions about my father. I found it odd, but answered truthfully. She also explained that even though Jim Reed was retiring, he had become involved again, because of Raúl's murder.

I told her about the stock certificates in the safe deposit box (the gun I didn't mention). And how I had visited Oaxaca with my father, once, when I was a kid. I played in the hotel pool, while he went galavanting around. I didn't see much of the town or meet many people. He bought me a palm leaf hat and a belt with a big silver buckle.

I told her everything I knew about his death, which wasn't much. She asked for Mom's current contact information, in case there was a lead they needed to follow. She had to rush back to the office, but agreed to meet me later for a drink.

+++

Late evening. We met at Evangelo's. I ordered a pint of Guinness. Jane asked for a "gin martini, up, with a twist."

She has a surprising directness, sincerity, which I find strange in a police investigator. She looks me in the eyes, steadily, with a probing—but not uncomfortable—intensity. She asked me to talk about Colibri.

I found myself telling Jane things I'd never confessed to C., or to anyone.

How, once, in an effort to analyze glottal stops, I made a surreptitious recording of lovemaking, specifically of the unique vocalizations C. made.

. . . *la la lor larlept lah-lo-la-ley*. . .

Later, I played that recording for a linguist colleague at school.

My recording C., without her knowledge, was treason enough. But to invade her privacy by playing the tape for this guy, was a complete betrayal. Maybe I was bragging . . . I don't know what I was doing.

"I didn't deserve her," I said, head in hands.

Jane sighed. Took a sip from her martini. Touched my arm briefly. Then, sitting upright, placing her hands palm up on the table, she began to unravel her own painful secret.

"This is the real reason I went into detective work," she said.

In college, pre-law, she had been raped in her dorm room. This was three o'clock in the afternoon. Her assailant wearing a white "Scream" horror-movie mask and wielding a knife came in through the window off the ledge. He gagged her and threw her violently to the floor. He held the knife to her throat. When it was over, she managed to knee him in the balls, at which time, he slashed her face (hence the scar near her mouth). Then he fled, escaping the way he had come in.

There was something familiar about him, but she couldn't place it. She wondered if she had unknowingly encouraged him, or insulted him in some way. Perhaps he was in her classes. He seemed to know her habits, and the habits of her roommate, who was always away at that time. He was never caught. The investigation didn't turn up any viable suspects. She underwent trauma counseling for years. The fact that the case was never resolved had tainted all her relationships with men. She rarely told anyone—not even her boss knew what had happened to her.

As she was telling me this, she pulled her hair down across her eyes. I saw the dark streaks among the light. Haunting image. A dream or memory. I felt myself breaking apart.

I put my arm around her shoulder. A fly alighted on the edge of my glass, proceeded to stroll boldly around the rim. I couldn't move. We sat there silently for some moments.

I surprised myself by inviting her to come see my new place.

I told her I had recently rented an airy, third-story apartment. The moon and streetlamps flood in my windows at night. I haven't any furniture, but we could sit on the floor and share some tea?

She said yes. This was miraculous.

— 7.16.2000 RELATIONS

Jane agreed to go with me to take Colibri's ashes to the ocean. She said, "Colibri feels like a sister to me." I was amazed by her open-heartedness toward someone she had never met.

I read aloud the poem C. had sent from Mexico, way back in 1996, before she consented to come north with me.

Hay tanta plenitud en esta hora
Tranquila entre los palmas de algún hado.

There is so much fullness in the present moment.

Tranquil between the palms of destiny's hands. — Jorge Guillén

I know Colibri spoiled me. As did my mother. I will now try to expiate my past privilege and stupidity.

What a pompous thing to say.

There is hope. Love breeds love they say. Something can be accomplished. Hindu scripture states that those who habitually speak the truth will develop the power of materializing their words.

I hope to find a way to make use of what I learned from C.

The trees, the grasses, always in motion . . .
Everything changes, nothing is ever still.
— 7.21.2000 RELATIONS

Heard, finally, from Colibri's teacher, Sr. Sarasco. He explained why it had taken him so long to write back. He said that he was still grieving. I understood completely.

He'd overturned every stone in search of the whereabouts of Raúl and his buddies. Found exactly nothing. Said it was as if Raúl had disappeared off the planet.

I had to write back, give him the gruesome facts surrounding Raúl's death in San Francisco.

Sr. Sarasco had advised Colibri to stay in Mexico. He had hoped to get her a scholarship to the University in Mexico City. He says he doesn't blame me for what happened to C., but he'd had a difficult time accepting "the fact of her departure to the United States, and then her subsequent death."

His words revived all my self-blame and misery.

He enclosed a story Colibri had written and sent to him a few years ago. She wrote it in Spanish. He told her, at the time, that he was starting up a literary magazine, asking her to send something for it. I've read it and re-read it. It's a beautiful story. Reveals some things about Raúl. Not particularly flattering to me. Makes me wonder about Jack. I guess he managed to see Colibri a time or two, while I was back in the States. Can't really blame him for trying.

I include the story here: Sr. Sarasco's English translation. — 7.29.2000 S.I.N.

+++

JILL WITH NO JACK
BY MARÍA CUERNO Y SAETA

On the way to the top of the mountain they discuss the well-documented phenomena of human beings spontaneously bursting into flames.

An *Izquierdo* weekly, left behind on the ferry, reported a recent incident. Out-of-work fishermen in an Argentinean coastal village, drinking heavily, got into a brawl. Then, they suddenly burst into flames. The twist in this story is the fact that two people had burst into flames at once:

> Old pals, very drunk, arguing over a boat, went into the street and tossed a few punches. The men started to laugh, then threw their arms around each other . . . when all at once the backs of their shirts began to smolder and a terrible stench of scorched flesh filled the air. There was a hissing sound, at first faint but growing louder and louder. A dark blue flame shot out the back of each, like twin blow torches . . . after a minute or so, there was nothing left but two piles of powdery ash.

She says: "Maybe it was because of the aguardiente the two men were drinking—an extremely potent distillate."

He says: "Some individuals possess a unique electro-dynamic system that funnels too much energy. But, it's true, some of the characteristic properties and reactions of alcohols are due to the unequal distribution of electric charge in the C-O-H portion of the. . . ."

He stumbles on a large, gnarly root.

She says, "There is also the volatile mix of anger and love as a contributing factor."

She glances at the field guide: *Lobelia polyphylium: deep red flowers and light green leaves combine to make large blossoms attractive to insects and useful medicinally.*

"Didn't the article say that the two men were blood related? Maybe they were too similar and easily inflamed in the same way at the same time."

"H-m-m-m, I don't actually believe a word of it." He steps into a muddy puddle.

This Jack is interested in accepted facts.

Fact: *Nicotiana tomentosa, a sprawling aromatic plant with large coarse leaves and pinkish white flowers—originally used medicinally, and as an insecticide.*

She feels the rise of the wind. Remembers words from the book David sent her: *Feelings can be grouped into four classes. The ones that depress. The ones that uplift. The ones that cause us to turn toward an object. Those that cause us to turn away.*

The wide, sandy stream bed is laced wall-to-wall with tiny yellow flowers. These flowers, she knows, contain a substance useful for relieving pain. And their seeds, mashed and steamed, aid in the dreaming.

The ones that depress: such as, despair, shame, remorse, grief, lack of self-respect.

She stands on a sloping incline, hillocks of volcanic rock to her left and right.

The ones that uplift: hope, pride, ambition, anticipation, pleasure, conscious acceptance of one's own power.

Far off up the valley, ragged mountains loom. Ocatillo and organ pipe cactuses stand firm, protecting their smaller brothers. Deposits of silt and minerals reveal precise drainage patterns.

There are the ones that cause us to turn toward: admiration, respect, love, affection, sympathy, a desire to be of service. . . .

David says he loves her and wants to help her. Can she believe him? The ground is littered with pea-sized gravel, formed from the combined forces of eons of glacial and seabed action. This mountain, says the guidebook, was pushed up from the ocean floor half a million years ago or more. This whole valley was once an ocean. Dry, now, on the surface, with vast reserves of water below. Nearly every inch gives rise to some kind of life, much of which cannot be seen from standing height.

And, feelings that cause us to turn away: fear, aversion, uncertainty, contempt, selfishness. . . .

A few bright orange flowers, large as a baby's hand, hang from the vine encircling a tree.

Some feelings, she realizes, are a mixture of emotions. *Feelings of defiance, suspicion, envy, and rage.* Such feelings cause us to turn toward an object but also carry a distaste or hostility toward the same.

She wonders about her brother. What place on this planet his feet have touched. She saw him kill a man once. He was ordered to do it by the group of monsters he called his friends. She was coersed into silence by her brother. Made to swear on the Bible by him. This brother, she once loved, is nowhere to be found. Her fear and concern for him know no bounds.

A certain type of passionate desire also involves a mixture of emotions: possessiveness, obsession, jealousy. . . come with intense feelings of worship, admiration, and genuine benevolence.

This Jack is attentive and responsible. Not like those clowns her brother used to bring home. But he is not the one she finds herself turning toward. He is not her Damasco, David, who also makes her turn away in fear for what he wants from her.

Jack has found a strata of rock that interests him. He removes his pick ax from its strap on the pack. His long fingers massage the polished steel. Small sounds of pleasure erupt from his mouth.

Brugmansia sanguinea, "*red angel's trumpet,*" *a perennial containing alkaloids, particularly scopolamine, ingestion of which can lead to violent disorientation, visions, and hallucinations.*

This mountain was inhabited by evildoers long ago. Her grandmother often told her the story. The demons arrived from deep in the sea and engaged in battles with archangels. The archangels were lazy. They had been seated too long on their golden thrones, idly playing video games. The demons wielded swords made from corn stalks and sugar cane. The demons wore no armor. Their skin was wet and porous. They knew no magic words. They could not talk with birds. Nonetheless, the demons won. Then, some ages passed, and the demons, too, got lazy. The archangels returned in force and the demons fled.

Jack is busy re-adjusting his pack. She keeps climbing. Climbing feels right. Something happens when you reach the summit. Always a different view than you imagined. . . .

Dusty from the excavation, Jack moves to catch up. Everything old interests him. Everything recorded, lodged in stone. His job is to sort, revise, quantify, and arrive at a new consideration, based on what has gone before.

Her job is somewhat different. She is to familiarize herself with the never-before, the cannot-have-been, the immeasurable, the hidden, the chthonian. This is not a field for investigation by human beings. It is the province of insects, planetary bodies, ancient trees, victims of catatonia. The dying.

She sees herself buried up to the neck in a history of bad solutions. The only way out is down or up. Up, too, is fraught with dangers.

"I'm thinking you might be right," Jack says, "that, if the event were true, the alcohol could have had something to do with it . . . but, I'm not sure about the emotions . . . emotions *are* electrochemically based, but people experience conflicting emotions every day."

She nods in agreement.

This Jack has intelligence. But he doesn't have access to her heart. She has kissed him, once, for fun. But this Jack is not like Julio, her first. Not like David, the one for whom she waits.

She holds something in reserve . . . the way her people know how to do. Now is not the time for thinking, for worrying. Keep moving, keep climbing.

Even if David does come back, she might decide not to go with him. He's unstable. Inconstant. Incomplete. This substantial mountain makes a better lover. The rocks are smooth beneath her feet and the roots of the trees cling to their graves of basalt. She pulls against gravity, climbing. What kind of person, descended from an old Mexican family, given an education, possessing brains and the grace of youth, what kind of person throws it all away for the first man who points to the moon.

Long ago they called her "puta."

Shame, remorse, defiance.

He said love, affection, marriage.

Fear, suspicion, pride.

Now David has schemed a way to bring her to the United States.

Feelings of hope and benevolence.

A cloud embraces the summit. The trail grows dim but her ardor for it increases as her breath becomes shallow and swift. Leafy habits of mind give thrust to her legs.

Courage, compassion.

Consciousness of one's worth and inner grace.

Jack glances side to side, a hundred paces behind her.

She is no Jill who comes tumbling after. If she falls it is because she wills.

+++

Last night, I had an omniscient vision that was so complete I peed the bed.

The vision was of myself disappearing and being completely replaced by an awareness. That's the only way I can describe it. In this awareness, there was a sort of Christ-like sacrifice of myself. A giving of myself completely.

I have never given myself completely to anything.

I used to wet the bed as a child. Dad whipped me with his belt.

Mom stood by and didn't try to stop him.

The experience last night seemed somehow the opposite of that.

I was rewarded for surrendering completely, by being given an extremely pleasurable awareness—an experience of the *absolute.* I don't know what else to call it.

I realized today—perhaps because of that experience—that what I had considered my strength was really my weakness. There is something I can do for myself, or the world. Maybe for Colibri. Hard to say. Yet I have resisted doing it. I know now that what I have to do, what I can do, will become clear, if I focus my intention.

Might I come to be as courageous as Colibri? Her courage in coming here with me, her courageousness in her protection of whatever it was she was protecting, whatever she was guarding or trying to release.

Soy hombre, verdad?

I am a man, true.

Cum auxilium ab alto.

With help from on high.

— 10.30.2000 NAMING

2001:
David Ambrose Gentry

It's been a while since I sat down and wrote in these notebooks. I mean actually wrote what's on my mind. Isn't that some kind of sin?

Continuing with my education. I am a (tentative) doctoral candidate and have been given two undergrad seminars to lead. Continuing, too, with a new kind of meditation: Instead of going inside myself, watching what goes on in my mind, I try to picture the entire globe of earth with all the beings on it, each with a destiny, each with a sense of being the center. So much movement, so much activity all across the globe, people pulsing and praying, striving and driving themselves insane, healing and yielding to desires, denying and trying to do things right.

I try to take it all in. Accept it all in the moment. Everything is as it should be in that instant. I hear the sound of a man washing a pan, a dog barking, sirens in the street, trees budding, grass growing, polar ice caps melting, bombs exploding.

Men more easily transcend matter. Make a familiar of the void. Perhaps it is our counterbalance to extreme self-centeredness.

Females create the world, make life, nurture things. Emotions closer to the surface.

It was Jane who convinced me to re-apply to UCB. We've been taking long hikes, exchanging stories. What a marvel she is. I want her to trust me. I want her in my life.

+++

Nothing is ever still. Apparent randomness is the truest fact we have to deal with. Any event, such as C.'s death, cannot be resolved, returned, reversed. I'm learning to live with it, to carry it with me at all times. Never forget, but not to dwell in it.

I'm attempting to find a way to incorporate her characteristics into my life. Her knowledge. Her essential nature becomes clearer to me each day, maybe even more than when she was alive. Gives me reason to get up in the morning.

If, at death, a soul is dispersed, a greater influence might occur than when the characteristics were limited to one small body. One small, nearly perfect, body.

Not sure if that thought is morbid or inspired. Maybe just John's "special" cigarettes talking again. Finishing the last of that. Quit smoking officially, in the morning. Goodbye rituals are sometimes good.

The concept of "total information"—God or Brahma—lends mathematical precision to the intuition that the world contains both order and chaos, interacting in unpredictable ways. To characterize our world in a manner that renders it compatible with "higher intelligence"—order increased at the expense of disorder, which is in direct opposition to what is expressed by the second law of thermodynamics: The entropy of the universe tends toward a maximum.

Tibetan monks create meaningful works of art made of colored sand. Of intricate precision. Then they intentionally randomize those carefully constructed works by sweeping them up and tossing them into the air or a river.

I sent a copy of the notebooks and diaries to G, my friend from back in sperm bank days. Perhaps to aid her in her dream research, but more importantly, I asked her to see if she can shed some light on Colibri's premonitions. The knowledge Colibri gained in dreams. G is now at Harvard Med School, Division of Sleep Medicine. She responded to Colibri's final dream entry.
— 2.13.2001

(excerpts from G's "rough notes")
Final dream begins with a chant and the urging of silence. Then the words: "Now it begins." I take these words to mean there is an acknowledgement (on the part of dreamer) that an important change is about to take place.

The radio ads reference drug companies and

agribusiness. The red cloth around dreamer's waist "drifting down like a bridal train" indicates a potential for life or death, coming from the area of the womb.

The dead sister and dreamer's first love both "disappear," reiterating the theme of separation. Objects: blanket—comfort, shroud; binoculars—insight, perception; school room clock—the time of youth has passed; bricks on hand truck—movement toward the inevitable; rubber wheels and Honduras might refer to her ancestors: the Maya developed rubber (balls), Honduras is a place where many indigenous tribes have settled.

Dry salt beds and stagnant lagoons: Is the life force diminishing or in danger?

Zócalo = modern town center built upon sacred ground of ancients (perhaps dreamer is being guided by ancestors). "The place where the two threads meet"—dreamer seems to be a seer, someone who moves delicately between worlds.

The boy & his grandmother seem to be supernatural beings, perhaps from the land of the dead: ice/dust/car "smooth as a coffin."

The grandmother helps dreamer in her passage

as she herself was helped by Colibri in San Francisco, years before (is this a fact?). Boy with fish is another spirit helper, points out that things are not what they seem. Firemen are "elementals." The scene turns gloomy: the "tiny yellow flowers" are significant as spots of intense color in a darkening world.

The boy's lenses: one dark and one clear, both are cracked . . . transition isn't going to be easy. Talk of botanicals: tobacco, vanilla . . . a kind of desperation sets in as they near the shoreline again. Where are the dreamer's loved ones? She must go alone . . . she asks, why? Is this old woman her ally or one who betrays her (as in earlier dreams).

Little girl riding on her brother's back—Colibri with her older brother? The childish world is now upside-down, however, the outcome remains fertile: a bat drops seeds, new plants start in deserts across the world.

The concrete ship seems definitive. She must board it by rowing out in her small boat, alone again. Important: dreamer is given a bag of seeds (the pearls from previous dream?) and warned not to share these with anyone, for now. Colibri's secrets will be kept close, will remain dormant, for a time. But will lead to other strong and powerful creations—the iron, silver, lead of the water. The knowledge of her ancestors will not be bought and sold but will grow with replanting in the proper time and place.

+++

After the response I got from my answer to the "Pharmco threat letter"—as Jane calls it—she decided she'd like to help me "privately investigate."

Then, came the sudden revelations in the news about some secret activities of my late father's corporation.

Less than a week ago, the scandal broke. Hexion Finance Group, a subsidiary of SLM Holdings, the corporation where my father was CEO before his death, was indicted in a covert operation promoting and laundering gun sales, specifically in the state of Oaxaca. Warring cartels were involved, and local groups of mercenaries, such as the GS group (*Guardia Silencio*) to which, we now believe, Raúl had belonged.

The fact is that my father's lifestyle, and my privileged upbringing, were largely funded by illegal acts—acts aggravating and condoning violence and disorder.

My anger, resentment, feelings of outrage, have finally galvanized me to act. I must uncover any and all connecting links between C.'s death, the Mortem Fendano fire, the pharmaceutical company battles, the arms smuggling, my father's lies and treachery, my own idle ignorance. The list is almost endless. But I will make a start.

If I can, I must take command of the fate of Colibri's land. Since I am legally her widower, Sr. Sarasco believes that the land goes to me, as Raúl had no heirs that anyone knows of.

About Jane: The first time she spent the night with me, I only held her and kissed her while she cried and cried. She hadn't been with a man for five years. The second time we slept together, we made love and made love so completely, I could still feel the motion the next day. She has decided to go with me to Oaxaca. I have tried to dissuade her. I question myself: Am I making the same mistake, bringing a loving innocent woman into a possibly dangerous situation? Direction south this time instead of north. I've tried to convince her to change her mind, but, for now, she is firm.

I don't know how I thought of it, just in the nick of time, but last month I sold my Hexion shares of common stock. That stock is practically worthless now with the breaking of the scandal. So, we've got a little nest egg to live on. I'm planning to repair Colibri's family home, make it livable. Figure out some kind of crop to grow there. Vegetables maybe, but Colibri always wanted to grow medicinal herbs on that land. Certainly would work as a "cover" for Jane and me. Also put us into the thick of it. Flush out the Pharmco advocates, perhaps.

Jane insists this investigation is *exactly* what she was trained to do. She always wanted undercover work. This is the kind of challenge she has been waiting for. She knows perfectly well how to behave like my "girlfriend" and gather information, without endangering herself or me. She has some CIA training that she neglected to tell me about, which I suppose might lead to more trouble, ultimately.

Jane also says she loves me. I don't know how or why I lucked out on this one, but I definitely feel the same way about her. I didn't know I could feel that way again.

Jane and I fly to Mexico City tomorrow, then on to Oaxaca. We will stay as long as we need to. Jane is officially on "furlough" for six months and that can be renewed and I have a one-year sabbatical from studies and teaching.

A package from Sr. Sarasco arrived earlier this week, including some photographs of C. and Raúl. Both were his students. He has promised to help any way he can. He mentions a letter he forwarded to C. from "a friend of the family," which came back to him unopened. In the "interest of confidentiality," he said, he will give me the letter when I see him.

This is possibly our first true lead.

I am closing these notebooks here. I'll begin a new document tomorrow, as soon as we board the plane.

For now, taking as my focus whatever inspires trust, feels true, and stimulates imagination.

— 3.19.2001 NAMING, S.I.N., RELATIONS

other books in the QUADRANTS SERIES

Quicksand
Robert Ashley

The Iron Boys
Thomas Frick

If Nothing Changes
L. K. Larsen

Q+1
short works from the
Quadrants Series authors

alere flammam

"I think POCKET BOOKS are perfectly excellent. Their format, type, etc., are admirable, and I feel sure they are doing a grand job in giving everybody in the country a chance to get a library together."
—Jan Struther, author of *Mrs. Miniver,* April 1943

"You never realized how much you can trust a BOOK—it has no wires or transistors or digital screen—it never breaks down, you don't have to pay a monthly fee to read it, no on/off switch, it's your friend in fact."
—Mark Weber, author of *Plain Old Boogie Long Division,* February 2011